The Murder Stone

Emma Hardy

Part One

Chapter One

Neath, July 1821

The only thought that Margaret had in that moment was to run. She was now forty miles from home and knew that if she didn't feel free now, she never would. Distance had to keep her safe though, didn't it?

The sun gave no sign of creeping through as her tired feet kept dragging, then rushing as she couldn't settle on a consistent pace. Every few seconds required a glance over her shoulder. Someone was there, behind her. She could feel it. The weight of her bag and clothes was forcing her to be slower. Men didn't have this misfortune. Pausing for composure, she hid in an alley to try and breathe. Her heart was thumping with no signs of slowing down.

These darkly lit streets would be no saviour to any predators. Margaret glanced across the street; certain she felt eyes upon her. A row of sheep heads in the butchers' window forced their eyes on her, fixated. She turned away. The cold crept over her, prickling her skin and stealing her breath. She must move on to daylight.

The town was empty, although voices could be heard. She didn't know where to turn, where to look. The darkness had robbed her of her sight. Moving shadows lurked in every corner. Was she alone? Margaret had to escape the follower. She held onto her bonnet and crossed the street. Footsteps rattled after her.

It would be hours until the hiring fair and walking the streets until the clock struck the appropriate hour would not do. Her feet stung, pinching her, almost taunting her with every extra step. Everything in this moment was working against her. A new start now felt like a ridiculous idea. Surely, she would be killed this night. Margaret let out a large sob and rubbed the tears away with the back of her hand. From the corner of her eye, she saw a tunnel so headed towards it. The tunnel smelt like a mixture of sweat and beer. As soon as she sat on the cold slatted ground, she heard a thump. It had a rhythm. Her mind told her to run, but her body could not, would not move, so she stayed frozen on the spot, trembling. A man. Her time was up. Stomp. Stomp. It was getting closer. She hid her face as she could not stand to look. The stomping quickened. He walked on by and doffed his hat to her.

'Miss.'

His walking stick hit the ground every second step he took. He left the tunnel without looking back.

Shortly after, a bird flew down the tunnel then back up. Margaret didn't like low flying birds, so sunk deeper into the edges of the tunnel.

She woke up to a small bird chirping at the tunnel entrance. She must have fallen asleep, using her bag as a pillow. Daylight soaked itself through the tunnel as she rubbed her eyes and blinked fast, trying to adjust herself to the new surroundings. She had survived the night, this time at least.

Chapter Two

St Catwg, March 2021

'Mummy, I learnt to read the word murder today.'

Tommy's mother, Angharad, jolted out of her trance on hearing such a horrifying word out of her innocent child's mouth. She had picked up Tommy from primary school; he was always excitable on the last day of the week but seemed particularly merry today as he was swinging his bookbag whilst skipping past the village churchyard. As Tommy was content, Angharad allowed herself to glance over towards the grave. Nothing could distract her in that moment; her surroundings were non-existent. Just her and that grave. The murder stone.

'Mummy, mummy, stop ignoring me, aren't you proud I can read long words now? My teacher said I am one of the top readers and I even got a sticker for it today.'

Angharad looked down at her son and forced a smile. She noticed Tommy becoming more excitable as they were closer to home - the bookbag was swinging more swiftly. She could distract him as soon as they were through the front door. He jumped up at her, stopping her from walking on. He patted his sticker and kept repeating the word 'Mummy!'

'Yes, Tommy, well done, keep going like that and you will be reading me your bedtime stories!' She tried to sound enthusiastic but could tell she sounded strained. Hopefully her son wouldn't notice. The grave and the word murder preyed so heavily on her thoughts that she just couldn't shake it off.

'Mummy, what does murder mean?'

'Something bad, Tommy, bad indeed.'

His mum opened the front door to the house. Thank God they were home. Tommy barged past her, nearly knocking her over and flew his bookbag across the room. He burst open his toy cupboard and settled down to play on the floor, making raspberry like truck noises. At least he had settled quickly. Tommy's mum felt shivery so went into the kitchen and poured a glass of water. What was it about that stone?

'Mummy, come and play this game with me, it'll cheer you up.'

She jumped again as Tommy's words bellowed into the kitchen. She went to sit on the floor with him by the window and play dumper trucks. Even though the graveyard couldn't be seen from their house, she felt drawn to turn her head every few seconds towards it, like someone waiting for a delivery to their front door that never arrives.

Chapter Three

St. Catwg, Neath, July 1821

Margaret Williams woke with new clarity that she had never had before. She knew she could never go back to her hometown again. She shuddered as she thought back to her old life. No more. It was time to look forward, not back. She had survived the night; she could continue to survive.

Having never visited Neath before, or seen it in daylight, she simply didn't know where to turn. Each direction revealed something brand new to her. People marched to the stalls they wanted in a systematic style. Margaret couldn't decide if it looked like a merry dance or a planned route with people sweeping in and out the streets in a jolly, yet busy fashion.

She stopped. What was that smell? A variety of meats were cooking and simmering away along the street. A pig was spinning on a stick under the heat, and she watched as it rotated. Her eyes still seemed to deceive her; performers in the street wriggling themselves into the most surprising shapes, children with their proud creations, trying to gain a little money. This town felt so alive to her, it was a whole new experience. She clasped her ears as market sellers shouted offerings of their latest sales and children pleaded with their parents for some pocket money.

This new world could not be more opposite to

the one life she'd ever known. She never expected to leave her village, or her parents, but there she was setting out on a new journey. Freedom. However much she ached for the view outside her bedroom or her family or some of her closest friends, who she had known her entire life, this would be better, safer. She could be anonymous in this area, invisible, even. Exactly what she needed after the past few weeks – to dust herself down and start again.

Her hair was stuck to her head, her legs were tired, but Margaret had walked the distance to the hiring fair. She stood waiting on the cobbled ground. Her feet shuffled and her fingers tapped against her dress. The town clock bell remained silent. Rows upon rows of girls and young women stood, and Margaret could feel her hopes depleting as another girl joined, then another. There were more girls lined up in that moment than there were girls in her entire village back at home. No, not home. She was currently homeless. How terrifying. She could not cope with another night like the last. It was a hot, stifling summers day in Neath. Surely it can't always be like this. She flapped the edge of her bonnet. It made no difference. Margaret recalled that when her friend Agnes had spoken to her, it had always been raining. Quite the contrast. She wiped her brow with her handkerchief. The bell rang, and a gentleman approached Margaret.

'Hello, Miss, can I take your name, please?' he said.

Margaret cleared her throat and smiled.

'Yes sir, I'm Margaret Williams, travelled from Carmarthenshire, sir.'

'Thanks Margaret, pleased to make your acquaintance, I am Mr. Richards, a farm owner of Gellia Farm, St. Catwg. Tell me, have you any experience on a farm?' he asked.

'Nice to meet you, sir. Yes, I grew up on a farm. Mostly spent time with the cows, sir. No one else wanted to work with them, but I do. Of course, all farmyard animals are lovely, sir. I'm a hard worker. I've worked on three farms so far.' Margaret finished, flustered.

'Well. I've heard enough.' Mr. Richards said sternly, then paused, and Margaret's face dropped as she thought she had ruined her one potential opportunity. All of the other girls were much younger, too. 'You have references, I assume, Miss Williams?' he asked.

She fumbled around in her small bag and held them out. She played with her hair. Mr. Richards took ages to read them. Seeing the papers from home made her think back in that moment. Two farm owners she'd worked so hard for. But no, she must not think backwards. This had to be a new life for her. She wanted to scream at him to hurry.

'I need a milkmaid and you're hired,' Mr. Richards exclaimed.

They shook hands. He had already picked up her luggage and was bounding down the road. She trotted behind to keep up with him, and the girls made a collective groan behind her as it was another opportunity missed for them.

Mr. Richards was a tall man with a large pot belly, like he'd eaten lots of his farm's produce all to himself. He was balding, with a big bulbous nose but had a warm face. Margaret was reminded of her own father and how opposite these two men looked. He had been friendly on the journey to Gellia Farm, making lots of small talk, describing her new home and the people in it.

Margaret noticed that he glowed as he talked about his son, Llewellyn, who he knew would take over the farm when the time was right. Margaret listened intently, trying to remember all the names he mentioned so she wouldn't look silly meeting so many people and forget who was who.

The second she arrived in St. Catwg, she knew she was home. A quaint little village on the edge of Neath with a church at its heart.

She made a note to herself to be acquainted with the vicar as soon as possible. Margaret had never seen such a variety of large houses, and slightly smaller ones, and teeny ones in one village.

Mr. Richards continued to take the role of village guide.

'Yes, this is one of the bigger families, the Tennant's, you'll hear lots about them in months to come, you know they are plotting an introduction of a canal. Mixed responses are coming from the village. I suspect it will never happen. You'll also notice further down another big house. The Mackworth's live there. Very well to-do. Don't let any of this intimidate you, though, Margaret. Most people in the village are like us, and we look after our own.' Was she one of them already? How lovely.

The walk into St. Catwg from Neath felt like a lifetime for Margaret. Her legs weighed heavier than her luggage. As they reached the church, Margaret hoped it wouldn't be much further, but when Mr. Richards shouted, 'We're about a mile up here,' she was pleased that the face she was pulling couldn't be seen by her new employer, who was bounding up the hill at a pace.

'Final stretch,' the words boomed out of Mr. Richards who was now strides ahead of her in his march up the hill.

Margaret nodded and forced an appreciative smile when she was secretly distraught that she hadn't yet reached her destination. Each farmhouse she walked past she hoped was Gellia, but they came and disappeared into the distance as she plodded on.

Mr. Richards stopped outside an entrance waiting for Margaret to catch up with him.

'I hope that you are fitter than this usually, Margaret, each day you need to make the walk from the field behind the church back up to this field here where the cows are.' He swung his arm around, pointing in lots of different directions which confused her.

'Sir, I apologise, I walked thirty miles to reach Neath yesterday. I am normally much better than this, I am so sorry.' Margaret hung her head. He smiled and patted her on the back.

'I'm teasing you, Margaret, but I didn't know you

walked far yesterday. Had I realised, I'd have brought a horse into Neath for us, but I didn't expect someone to have travelled as far as you. I'll be kind to you tomorrow and you can have the day off and start the day after. It's important you feel settled and ready for work.'

'Why, thank you, sir. I won't let you down.'

They walked a little further down a windy, dirty mud track. Margaret's feet relaxed as the final few steps were on flat ground. It appeared that Gellia Farm had a lot of land and it stretched as far as she could see. She liked the small garden area near the farmhouse front door, but it was untidy, unkept and uncared for. Margaret made her way to the back of the farmhouse.

The route she had walked suddenly made sense as she saw the church far down below and a few people who were simply going about their day. As she squinted, she noticed that the gravestones were facing away from the farm and that comforted her. She wouldn't have liked the dead to be watching her at the house. Margaret saw the vicarage and wondered what the vicar might be like. She pondered that they were nearly always elderly gentlemen, balding, with a large stomach. Maybe she would be surprised. She hoped so. There was a gentle buzz floating around her, and Margaret watched as the bees flew from flower to flower. A butterfly landed on the stone wall she was leaning against. It had bright blue and red colours reflecting on the wall as the hot sun persisted beating down on the farm. Margaret tilted her head up to the sunshine and took a deep breath. The butterfly daintily fluttered off the wall and lowered itself towards St. Catwg.

The farmhouse was a large white house with few windows. Mr. Richards had left the large wooden front door wide open for her. Margaret's eyes had to adjust from the bright glare outside into the dark parlour and kitchen area. It was a typical farmhouse that Margaret was familiar with. Beams on the ceilings supported the structure of the house, there were a couple of windows in the large open room and lots of furnishings inside to make it feel homely.

The house looked to be more of a dumping ground and Margaret smiled to herself as she realised it needed a woman's touch to turn this house into a home. Dust and dirt lurked in every corner and on the hard floor. Crumbs of food were left sprinkling tables and work tops. Farm related objects and bits of machinery were stood like oddly shaped statues in walkways. Margaret thought back to the market earlier and thought she saw one of the performers doing a similar shape to how this object stood. As she was shown the direction of her bedroom, she nearly knocked an unidentified tool over and blushed in embarrassment. Margaret had never before seen such a dirty and messy house, but she was particularly surprised at herself that she didn't care. Thoughts went back to the morning when she panicked that she would not have a room for the night. She dropped herself on to the bed and sighed in satisfaction. Not only did she have a bed, but she also had her own room. Margaret had been convinced she'd have to share with someone. Settling into her room, she swung her legs over the edge of the bed and kicked off her well-worn shoes. She wriggled her toes and scrunched up her feet. That felt good. Margaret wondered if she might get away with a quick lie down, but Mr. Richards and the farm had other ideas. As she started to close her eyes, Mr. Richards poked his head around the corner.

'Come, Margaret. Time for food.'

She nodded and took a quick peek out of her small bedroom window. The butterfly had re-joined her and was sat on the sill on the outside of the house. Margaret studied it with her head against the window as if trying to reaffirm that it was the same one and came to the conclusion that it most definitely was.

She hadn't realised how hungry she was until she was sat at the table. It reminded her of how appetising the pig smelt earlier in the day in Neath and her stomach growled. Llewellyn, the eldest son approached her, shook her hand and stared at her.

'Welcome to Gellia, Miss Williams.'

Margaret felt herself blush as his blue eyes beamed at her. She became aware that she was almost falling down with fatigue but sat up straight, still smiling at the young man who was her employer's son.

David, a farm worker, who also lived at the farm approached her and Margaret noticed that Llewellyn and Mr. Richards looked cautious. David proceeded to waggle his fingers and make a few grunts. Mr. Richards was about to step in when Margaret answered straight back in sign language with, 'Hello David, I'm Margaret, how are you?'

Mr. Richards and Llewellyn looked at each other as Margaret spelled out her name with such precision. David signed back with the thumbs up, followed with a thank-you sign, starting with his hand at his mouth and pointing it downwards. Margaret smiled as she saw that David had tears that had not managed to spring out of his eyes.

'Margaret?' Mr. Richards asked.

'Yes?' came the nonchalant reply.

'Where did you learn to do that?' He sounded stunned.

'Oh. What, signing? We had a deaf boy in the village I was from, Peter. No one bothered to speak with him, so I spent time with his family to learn how to sign so he'd feel less left out.' She shrugged this story off, not thinking it was a particularly significant thing.

Mr. Richards wouldn't let this drop. 'You are only the third person to speak to him directly for years, Margaret. You do not know the impact that you will have made on him. This is so important.'

Margaret brushed this aside, 'Glad I can help.'

Again, the men looked at each other.

Margaret was smiling on the inside. Her mousy hair was lank,

loose from the travelling, and she hadn't yet had a chance to tidy herself up. No one minded. Margaret then remembered Mr. Richards had unusually given Margaret the next day to settle into the village before starting work. She used that warm smile again to grin at her new employer.

After the meal, the house was keen to get to know her, and questions were fired at her from everyone. Everything was answered truthfully and honestly; she thought she might feel overwhelmed, but she didn't. Margaret secretly loved the attention. It felt liberating to see new faces, new characters. Her life had previously felt grey, whereas Neath was bringing her life into colour. There was so much laughter that her freckled cheeks hurt. She saw that Llewellyn was already showing himself to be protective over her, gently patted her shoulder every so often. As a quiet fellow, Margaret noticed that he wasn't an active member of the conversation but responded in all the right places and was captivated by Margaret every time a word was uttered. She shined in this company.

Thoughts returned to what Mr. Richards had said earlier about David, and Margaret had made an effort to include him in the conversation, signing where she could and making him feel a part of the conversation. All the farm staff were infatuated with Margaret in an instant. David signed something funny and she threw her head back and laughed, the others not quick enough to catch the joke.

It had been such an engaging evening that candles were using up their last wax. Margaret felt strange lying in her new bed. She stared up at the beamed ceiling for a while before her eyes fell shut with tiredness. She already ached for this to be her forever home. Exhausted from all the excitement, she got to sleep quickly and remained still for the night.

Chapter Four

St. Catwg, July 1821

After an excellent night's sleep, Margaret was all set to get to know the village and its inhabitants before she started work. She wanted to put the extra day into good use. As she reached the bottom of the hill, she spotted a little old lady pottering about in the garden of her terrace house, near the church.

The old lady spoke, 'Good morning, lovely day for walking around the village, isn't it?' She stopped close to the unknown lady and looked up to the sky with one hand at her brow to see more clearly from the sun's glare.

'Good morning to you, too, it is indeed a fine day. I'm the new milkmaid, up at Gellia Farm, I will suppose that you know it. My name is Margaret. And you are Mrs…'

'Evans, dear. Yes, I know it. I heard Mr. Richards was going to the hiring fair yesterday so expected to see a fresh face. Although I never heard about what happened to the previous one before you, but I'm guessing that hasn't been shared with you, either. Are you not working today? You seem old for a new milkmaid.'

Mrs. Evans stopped and took her time and eyed the girl most curiously and stared for what felt like an eternity at Margaret, who stared back, unsure what to do or say next.

Mrs. Evans was bent over, almost crooked in her

old age. Her grey hair was tidied immaculately beneath her hat, and she was well presented, thought Margaret as she waited for the old lady to speak again.

'Have you met our vicar yet? Reverend Isaac is a wonderful gentleman and much loved in this community. I assume you are a church goer?' Again, she eyed Margaret up and down.

'Yes, of course. I was on my way there. Mr. Richards has given me the day to settle in before work tomorrow, so I want to meet everyone that I can.' Margaret smiled warmly, restraining her enthusiasm as she could tell that the other woman would be quick to judge. Mrs. Evans, however, had clearly had enough of this awkward exchange.

'Well, enjoy the village, we're a friendly group, close-knit, look out for each other. I hope you'll settle in. Not like the last one they had. Goodbye.' Mrs. Evans left a confused Margaret as she banged her walking stick and stumbled her way back into the house, slamming the door shut. Margaret jumped at the loud noise. She couldn't stop thinking what a strange conversation she had taken part of and hoped that the rest of the community were going to be more friendly!

She crossed the road and saw the church that stood on the main thoroughfare, slightly elevated. The front faced into the core of the village, but Margaret noticed that from the back of the church, she could see the hills that led back to Gellia Farm. The church, although not exactly *in* the heart of the village, Margaret knew would *be* the heart of the village. It was its centre piece, there at the beginning and the end of each villager's life. It was old in appearance, and looked in a desperate state of repair, but Margaret liked how it looked. She peered around the back and saw her field of cows would be situated right behind it. Margaret now knew her route to work and liked that it involved being so close to the church. The church entrance looked so inviting. It was empty as she entered and she couldn't spot anyone in the nave or the vestry, so she shouted a 'Hello?' into the atmosphere. It echoed around her but there came no reply. She sat down in the church to collect her thoughts. She prayed. Margaret finally let her thoughts drift back towards home. Knowing the family routine so well, she knew her mother and father would be busy on the farm. Her mother would be with the pigs, her father with the cows. The other women would be collecting their water and having a catch up with latest family news. Margaret's eyes started to glisten and she wiped them. It was not proper to show emotion in public.

With an emotional shudder, Margaret realised that she had to let the past go. Everything around her stayed quiet and still so she rested a few moments more and then continued her tour of the church. Its candles were lit, flowers arranged nicely and some plaques on the wall, carefully arranged, told the church's history. Margaret, for the first time in a long time, felt at peace. This village, this church, everything around her felt like it had a stillness. Keen to embrace her surroundings, she took a deep breath, exhaled and exited the church to inspect her cow field.

Reverend Isaac had seen Mrs. Evans interrogating what looked like a new lady into the village. Normally he would have approached them, but he noticed Mrs. Evans with a stern look in her eye, so decided on this occasion to avoid what looked to be an awkward encounter. Rumour had it that Gellia Farm were after a new milkmaid, although this one looked older than the last. He suspected he'd meet her soon enough. As Reverend Isaac was leaving his vicarage, coincidentally, he bumped into Mr. Richards of Gellia Farm.

'Hello, Vicar.' Mr. Richards was particularly happy and bouncy this morning.

'Morning, Mr. Richards. I say, did I spot your new milkmaid skipping down the hill this morning? I saw a fresh-faced bonny girl looking a little flustered at the wrath of Mrs. Evans and wondered, with it being the hiring fair yesterday, if she was connected to you?' he enquired.

'Yes, Vicar, that's our Margaret. She has a lot of farming experience. She's travelled all the way from Carmarthenshire, she said.' Mr. Richards replied.

'Oh, that's a long way, isn't it. Well, I know we'll make her welcome. I'm sure Mrs. Evans will warm to her after she sees her in church a few times - I assume she's a church goer at least?' Reverend Isaac asked.

'Yes, she said the first thing she wanted to do was

to become acquainted with the church and its vicar, so I'm sure you'll be meeting her soon,' Mr. Richards said. He added, in hushed tones, 'Our Llewellyn took a shine to her, Vicar, who knows, maybe next July we'll be scheduling a wedding, or a christening or both.' He rubbed his hands with glee.

Reverend Isaac, trying to curb his surprise, answered, 'Well, that would be some delightful news, wouldn't it? It's been too long since we've had a wedding here, so that would be a lovely piece of news from the village. But let's not get ahead of ourselves. Please send Llewellyn my best wishes, and I'm sure I'll meet our new villager soon.'

The two gentlemen shook hands before they parted and headed in opposite directions. Mr. Richards walked off whistling some summery sounding tune. The vicar was left wondering about what Margaret must be like to make Llewellyn sparkle. That man rarely looked up from the floor.

Margaret was embracing the sun in the field that was soon to be her workplace. She had settled quickly into the village and loved it there. Her memories of Llangynderyn were fading at a speedy pace. This was her forever home. She knew it. Margaret thought back to last night and recalled how Llewellyn looked at her. He really had looked at her. Thinking back to that memory, she blushed. She remembered his broad shoulders, rugged features, strong jaw. Margaret dreamed about snuggling into those muscular arms. No, she must not go there. Before the awkward feelings could return, she dusted her long skirt down and adjusted her hat. It was time to find the vicar.

Margaret climbed uphill through the field and marshland, the sun still beaming down on her warmly. The village was so tranquil and quiet – the complete opposite to the volume of people she saw at Neath market only yesterday. Margaret reached the top and followed the path along the back of the church, heading back towards its entrance. At the entrance stood a portly man, mostly bald with hair tufts either side. He looked a happy enough fellow.

Margaret approached him, 'How do you do, Reverend? I assume you are our vicar anyway, you definitely are wearing the right uniform; oh, here I go blabbering on again.' Catching herself being immature, she paused for breath and smiled serenely. Some sort of awkward curtsy was presented to the vicar. They shook hands. She continued.

'Margaret Williams, sir. The new milkmaid at Gellia Farm, from Carmarthenshire, sir, made the journey only two days ago. I will be frequenting your services and look forward to meeting all the other parishioners in due course. Mr. Richards and his family have made me feel welcome, and well, the church is such a beautiful place of worship.' She stopped. Reverend Isaac looked bemused as he caught her finding herself in such a fluster, embarrassed at how she had rambled on.

'My name is Reverend Isaac and may I extend to you a warm welcome on behalf of the village. We are small but mighty and have a loud voice when we need to. I look forward to seeing you more as you attend the services and am sure we'll see each other often as you make your daily route past the church.' He was friendly, approachable. But he was an old, portly man, after all. Margaret smiled again.

'My religion is important to me, Reverend Isaac, and I am so pleased I have such a wonderful place of worship on my doorstep. I feel privileged. I assume Mrs. Evans is a regular also?' Margaret enquired.

'Ah. You've had the pleasure.' He put his arm around dear Margaret and she felt immediately comforted. 'Don't worry about her, her bark is worse than her bite. She'll see you in church once or twice, realise you take religion seriously and then you will have a friend for life.' Margaret wasn't wholly convinced but decided not to pursue the matter any further.

Putting on a relieved face, she said, 'Oh, you do know how to reassure a member of your congregation, Reverend, thank you so much.'

'If you can excuse my mess, my dear, would you like to have a longer chat in the vicarage, Miss Williams? I can talk you through the day-to-day life of St. Catwg and we can get to know each other better?'

She felt herself blush – this was becoming a far too common experience around the men of this village.

'Oh, Margaret, please Reverend Isaac, no need for formalities, I hope we can become firm friends.'

They headed towards his house, Reverend Isaac leading the way. Margaret saw Mrs. Evans, back in her garden, staring at the two of them. She couldn't help but stare as she saw Mrs. Evans' walking stick slam against the floor with force. Margaret overreacted with a laugh, knowing how much it would irk Mrs. Evans and wondered had the other woman ever received an invitation into the vicarage before? Probably not. Margaret strutted into the shabbily grand house, looking like she owned the place – and gave a generous wave over to Mrs. Evans before going in. Reverend Isaac followed Margaret's wave before ushering Margaret inside.

Margaret's job had started well, and she had spoken to lots of villagers but could barely remember anyone's name which she felt slightly guilty about as they all remembered her. On her morning walk she'd be greeted with lots of familiar faces with plenty of 'Good Morning Margaret!' 'How do you do, Margaret.' 'Miss Williams, hello!' from the children. Despite being a milkmaid, she felt like the most famous woman in the village. She loved her job. Margaret had been an animal lover ever since she was a child. Growing up on a farm and surrounded by wildlife, she had a curious mind with animals and felt comfortable and happy around them. Gellia Farm was a welcoming and happy home. Mr. Richards had barely paid her any attention as he was always out and about speaking to this person or that person, and socialising. It felt good to feel trusted from day one. Most of her nights so far had been getting to know Llewellyn.

He was extremely shy, but each night he relaxed and opened up a little bit more. Margaret had that way about her, she could talk and talk, and everyone soon spoke to her like an old friend. She knew Llewellyn would take a little bit more work than most, but she'd get there. She saw the signs. The village was the fresh start she needed. Keen to keep David included too, Margaret ensured that they had a signed conversation daily and passed messages frequently. He, too, looked at her in awe.

Mrs. Evans, however, was getting angrier by the day and her antipathy towards Margaret was heightened rather than lowered. Everyone she bumped into, she'd enquire their opinion of the young woman.

'Have you met Margaret that new milkmaid?' she asked.

'Yes, what a cheery young lady to have in the village, I think she's caused a stir amongst the young men of the village if truth be told, Mrs. Evans.' Mr. Jones replied, merrily.

'Quite a stir, I say, quite a stir indeed. She needs to know her place and realise she's here for the cows and not the men.' Mrs. Evans scowled at the thought of all the young men chasing after this woman.

'Oh, dear, Mrs. Evans, I think Margaret is being kind and the men are falling at her feet. She's innocent and naïve!'

Mrs. Evans realised that Mr. Jones was giving her a telling off and remained quiet as he continued. 'Give her a chance, I thought your faith would encourage you to do so.' Mr. Jones smirked at Mrs. Evans, who was now more flustered.

'My faith? My faith? How dare you, Mr. Jones, it is unfair to bring my faith into this conversation. Good day to you.' She swiftly marched off muttering and mumbling to herself.

Chapter Five

Neath, March 2021

Women across the UK walked silently. This was not a march, or a protest, but a vigil. A peaceful vigil. Yet again, a woman had been killed at the hands of a man. This one stung more than most. A policeman. Someone you are meant to trust and feel safe around. There came no reassurances from anywhere that this would be properly addressed or tackled, now or in the future. Women remained vigilant, not wanting to walk alone in the dark, or sometimes walk alone at all. They'd been cat called, verbally abused, flashed at, groped and abused. Mentally abused. Physically abused. Sexually abused.

This vigil stood for all women. Every single woman that had suffered at the hands of a man. Every single woman that had felt unsafe. Every devastated family that permanently suffered loss at the hands of a man. Women were angry, enraged even. But still protested peacefully as a memorial.

She was just walking home.

Whilst London was featured on the news, local vigils occurred throughout the country. One particularly small one happened in Neath. The local Neath women wanted to act. They met outside Neath Castle gates. There was only a handful of women, but numbers didn't matter. Solidarity did. It had started as a social media invite and soon a chat got going. They meant no harm, just wanted to do something, felt compelled to do something.

It was a light evening and with safety in numbers, the group of ten walked around the town of Neath. They shared stories of times they felt scared of men, but also funny stories as they giggled together, discussed work, their family and friends and who knows who, or who might know who. They built a sisterly bond on that walk. They walked past the local supermarket, the travel agents, a local café, up past the local theatre and cinema hall and towards the gardens. They lit a candle in the gardens and sat in the pavilion, retrieving their flasks from their rucksacks to sip a warm drink. Although everyone teased Sheila that hers must have been brandy the amount she babbled on after only a few sips. Her confidence grew significantly.

'You know where we need to go ladies, don't you?' It was a dramatic voice that she put on, but the girls giggled and humoured Sheila, who incidentally took another sip of the unknown liquid. Unknown to the girls anyway.

'We need to visit the stone,' Sheila muttered.

'The stone?' Tina asked.

'Yes, the stone.' Sheila nodded to confirm but the ladies hadn't a clue what stone she was referring to.

'What stone, Sheila?' Tina asked again, a little less patiently this time.

'The murder stone.' Sheila said.

'Oh, the one in St. Catwg?' Beth piped up.

'Yes,' Sheila said.

'That's a good point, actually,' Beth replied.

'What's the murder stone?' asked Kelly.

'Kelly, of course, you are new to Neath, so probably don't know about this. In the Victorian times, or thereabouts, a women was strangled as she was walking home and, in anger, a prominent member of the village paid for a gravestone reading 'murder' at the top of it, to haunt who they thought did it.'

'Wow. That sounds so spooky. To the murder stone I say, then,' Kelly asserted. 'If another woman was murdered whilst walking home, all the more reason for us to go, I would think.'

The girls gathered up their belongings and slid their arms through their rucksack straps. Kelly blew out the lit candle, the small trail of smoke dissipating into the wind. The night had taken an unexpected turn, but the more Sheila thought about this, the more she realised the direct parallels between current events and the murder stone girl.

They were just walking home.

The walk to St. Catwg was only about a mile but as they were taking their time, this was about a twenty-minute walk. Kelly, however, got a bit carried away at seeing a fast-food place and immediately rushed in and bought a double cheeseburger with fries and a large strawberry milkshake. The ladies didn't mind that this had delayed them only a short while, as long as they could pinch a chip, or two. Sheila had settled down, too, much to the relief of the other women. At different points of the journey, the women all commented how good it felt to walk in the evening. They felt the safety in their numbers. Although Neath was a generally harmless place, a woman alone wherever she was in the world, would always feel the danger, even if there was nothing to fear.

They approached the graveyard.

The walk had revived Sheila somewhat. She threw her arms out in front of the stone and bellowed, 'Here she is, then, the murder stone girl.'

Beth giggled. 'Only in Wales could such a solemn moment get humorous. Kelly, you'll soon realise that the Welsh like to deal with difficult and serious subjects through humour.'

Kelly nodded and got out her torch as it was beginning to get dark, and read the stone in a murmur, not realising that anyone else was listening in.

'1823, to record MURDER. The stone was blah, blah, blah, oh, this goes on a bit. Margaret Williams, a native of Carmarthenshire – ooh, Sheila, she was from your way originally, Carmarthen way - living in service in the Parish, who was found dead with marks of violence on her person in a ditch on the marsh below this churchyard of Sunday the fourteenth of July 1822.' Kelly's words got to more of a mumble as she read on that her words became inaudible. Those ladies who were listening, joined her to finish reading the final few words on the

stone. Sheila was sat on a bench nearby, seeing their reactions and soaking up the atmosphere. She hadn't expected to end up in a graveyard tonight, but she had enjoyed it. Sheila took another swig of her drink.

'What do you think, girls?' she shouted across to them.

Kelly replied. 'I can't believe it. Down this marshland, a murder happened around two hundred years ago. Yet two hundred years later, we are still unable to walk home safely. Isn't that completely and utterly devastating?'

The word 'devastating' hung in the air for what felt like minutes between the women. This is exactly why they were there. The laughter, the jokes, the humour settled down as the women circled the grave to pay tribute. The candle was re-lit on the grave with the shadow flickering on the gravestone's haunting words. The women stayed silent and had a solemn few minutes at the grave, remembering why they were there and thinking of the thousands of women, who had lost their lives to the hands of a man. It felt all too real being there at that stone.

Local historian Sam Honey was walking home from The Crown Inn when he saw the bunch of women with a candle surround the murder stone grave. The vigil. How unfair that women couldn't walk freely and feel safe, just as he was doing. At least they caught the murderer this time, somehow that helps even though a life has been lost. It was so unfair that the murder stone girl never had seen justice for her murder. To this day, the village never could provide that certain answer. Was it the boyfriend? It seemed likely. But then how didn't it unravel that way? If only there was a way to try and rectify this. But he was a historian, not a detective. The need for a resolution to this after nearly two hundred years would never leave him. But the path always ran cold.

She was just walking home.

Chapter Six

Coombe Lodge, August 1821

Mr. Tennant called a meeting. He'd invited dukes and lords from the surrounding Neath area to come together to listen to his proposal. Proud of his home, Coombe Lodge, he had his staff create a meeting room for Friday afternoon, midday, prompt. All of the men had confirmed their attendance and were rubbing their hands with glee at a potential business opportunity. The dining room was laid out with lavish food and plenty of drink, to encourage a social afternoon. Mr. Tennant raised an eyebrow whilst pondering how drunk these men might have to get to say yes to his ambitious proposal.

One by one, the men were introduced by Alice, a maid, into the main room. Mr. Tennant had worked closely with Alice to get her to enunciate her words as her accent was wobbly at best.

'Mister B-Bullins, sir.' It appeared she was now too far the other way, trying too hard and rolling her words around her tongue instead of speaking naturally. Mr. Tennant rolled his eyes then shooed her away. She returned quickly with the next gentleman to arrive.

'Lord Beaufort, sir.' Again, Mr. Tennant shooed her out promptly but said nothing at her attempts to speak what she would call 'proper'. The spacious room had the sun entering it from the windows of the East Wing. Mr. Tennant had made the conscious decision to keep all of his windows and pay the window tax. He thought houses with any boarded-up windows looked tatty and cheap, and that was not what Coombe Lodge was about. The beer was already flowing into the gentlemen who had arrived early. Mr. Tennant's father's portrait hung behind him and stared down at proceedings. The likeness was so similar that a couple of the gentlemen round the table declared it must have been Mr. Tennant himself who graced the wall. Seeing as his father was ten years older than his current age when that portrait was painted, Mr. Tennant tried to shrug off becoming offended, particularly as he needed these men onside.

Alice made her final declaration of attendance and then scurried out the room. As she shut the door, she re-adjusted her clothes and sighed. She felt so stupid trying to say those words as Mr. Tennant had taught her. What he wanted her to do didn't sound right. She'd tried too hard to impress him but had clearly failed. Alice thought back to Mr. Bullins's arrival and wanted to scream. He had surprised her after he dropped a coin on the floor, and as she went to pick it up for him, he pressed himself against her and kept her bent over for a longer amount of time than appropriate.

She tried to not let it upset her but as she stood back up and went to pass the coin back to him, he slid it into the pocket of her apron which was tied around her waist and muttered, 'Keep it.' He then patted her backside as she tried not to wail. Choking back the tears she had managed a 'Thank you, sir, very kind.'

As soon as all the expected gentlemen had arrived, she ran to her bedroom to sob. The housekeeper was quick to spot this and followed her to her bedroom banging on the door to discuss.

With all men seated at the table, Mr. Tennant began his thoroughly prepared speech.

'Gentlemen, I appreciate your time today. Please do enjoy the beer and food prepared by my excellent kitchen staff and welcome to Coombe Lodge. I am sure you are wondering why I have brought you all here today. This is to bring you in on what I believe will be the making of Neath. I wish to build a brand-new canal and would like to invite you all to be investors. Whilst you think about it, I'll tell you my plans. According to my careful calculations, I believe that this canal would carry around one hundred thousand tons per year and generate eight thousand pounds in income annually.' Mr. Tennant paused for dramatic effect of these numbers, then carried on with his pitch.

'It would be eight to nine miles long and run towards Swansea docks. I believe this route would give us a particular advantage and provide a better shipping point for us, than in anywhere around the Neath area.'

The men around the table thus far did not look convinced. Mr. Bullins was the first to express his concern.

'Presumably you want some of my land, Tennant?' He spat out these words. Mr. Tennant chose his words carefully.

'Well, yes, a small portion of your land in Skewen would be required here to accommodate it travelling towards Swansea docks.' Before Mr. Bullins could ask any more, Mr. Tennant disappeared out of the room to gather up some drawings made of the proposed plans to show where would be affected. He returned, placing them on the table and rolling them out. The men loomed over these drawings and said nothing for what felt to Mr. Tennant to be a long time. Lord Beaufort broke the silence.

'Wouldn't it be more preferable to extend Neath canal as it already exists and could easily attach to better places?' The other men murmured in agreement. Mr. Tennant was still optimistic that he could win them over.

'Gentlemen, why, you aren't thinking grand enough here. This will be ours to profit from, not others trying to steal our hard-earned money. Ours.' He patted the closest men to him on the back. They looked at him and then back down at the plans saying nothing. Mr. Bullins declared his position.

'Thanks for the hospitality, Tennant, but you aren't having my land or my money for this unpractical dream of yours. Good day.' He left the room without a glance back. He had left sooner than expected. The other men did not take long to follow Mr. Bullins out but were slightly less aggressive in turning down the proposal. They wished Mr. Tennant well but refused to support any investment. Within only minutes Mr. Tennant was left staring alone at his own plans and kept sipping his beer. He'd prove them wrong. He'd fund it himself. He didn't need anyone else.

Chapter Seven

Mrs. Evans' House, August 1821

Mrs. Evans was following her usual daily routine. She had her walk around the village (this was instilled in her from an early age by her father, who told her that under every circumstance she must do a walk around the village every single day). As a child she rolled her eyes and skipped along, ignoring him. But in later years, she could see exactly what he meant and endeavoured to listen to her wise father's advice. After her leisurely stroll around the village, Mrs. Evans, if it was sunny, would sit outside in her front garden area and watch the passersby. Her and her family had been in the village for years, and there was rarely a face she didn't recognise. Even into old age, her mind was sharp. Slower, but sharp.

She hooked her walking stick onto the side of the chair and waited for the village to wake. Mrs. Evans smiled thinly as she always heard the children first. Although she found the noise joyous, it was bittersweet. God had not blessed her and Mr. Evans with children. She felt sorrowful, thinking back to those days where she realised her house would not be full of voices of innocence, and motherly love she had to give. Still, she couldn't complain. She loved her life in the village. Mrs. Evans told herself that God had wanted her all to Himself. Selfish man. But she remained loyal. Her chin wobbled thinking back to those thoughts, her jaw hanging loose and her mouth moving as though speaking, though she wasn't. The curly grey hair never moved from her head even though Mrs. Evans was rarely still. The rest of her body, like her jaw and mouth, seemed to make involuntary movements often. Her hands shook regularly; her ankles unsteady. She was most comfortable sitting down and felt the sun was her best medicine. And prayer. The children were now zooming past her and called to say hello to her, 'Morning, Mrs. Evans', 'How do you do, Mrs. Evans', 'Lovely weather we are having Mrs. Evans!' The words and echoes chimed around her. She replied cheerily to every single child and was glad of the young company, all be it for only seconds as they continued to play, pretending to ride on imaginary horses and canter away leaving her in the dust behind them.

The parents wearily followed next, barking instructions at the children.

'Slow down, George', 'Don't go bothering Mrs. Evans, Victoria', 'Stop shouting, Henry.' They waved at Mrs. Evans, who by now had a blanket around her knees as she felt the fresh morning air around her legs. Seeing this daily routine made her feel like she was a part of this village. She was less active in the village now, but she hadn't been forgotten. A smell caught in Mrs. Evans' nose and as her face crinkled up, her nose twitching like a rabbit's, she let out a large sneeze. She grabbed her handkerchief, wiped herself down and placed it back underneath the blanket. It was then she saw Margaret fleeting down the hill to cross the track to the cow field, as she did every morning. Margaret was spritely and full of joy. She waved and greeted Mrs. Evans, who was still a bit disorientated from her sneeze. Mrs. Evans made a polite nod to Margaret, but no more. She still was not sure about that girl. Did not trust her. She clearly had an intuition with the cows, though, as they followed her every step and did exactly as she instructed every morning. Mrs. Evans thought that Margaret looked most at ease and happiest when with her herd.

Next, most unusually, followed Mr. Richards bounding down the hill.

'Good morning, Mrs. Evans,' he shouted across the track, doffing his farmer's flat cap.

'Good morning to you. Mr. Richards. I say, this is a surprise, I don't usually see you on mornings like this, is everything all right?' Leaning to one side, she pushed herself off her chair and propped herself up to stand and speak to him. Her handkerchief and blanket fell down to the ground and Mr. Richards rushed to pick these up and place them on her chair. She dusted down her black shawl and skirt.

'Thank you, Mr. Richards.' He stared before deciding to answer her question.

'Ah yes, I am heading into Neath to pick some things for the farm. I was going to send Llewellyn, but I couldn't find him this morning, so off I go.' Mrs. Evans was intrigued.

'Well, where is he? I haven't seen him this morning.' She squeezed her hands into fists. They had become stiff since she had been sitting outside. Her eyes looked up at Mr. Richards.

'I don't know, Mrs. Evans. He wasn't in the farm, unless he's wandered off to a piece of land, I wouldn't have seen him. I don't usually miss him, though, do I, he's a tall one.' Mrs. Evans saw Mr. Richards smile at his own joke but was certain she saw sadness and concern behind his eyes. Still, it was not for her to get involved, at least not yet anyway. She could always speak to Llewellyn about it when he returned.

'Well,' Mrs. Evans said, shrugging her shoulders, 'if I see him, I'll tell him not to disappear again for you. Let me know if I need to start a search party, though.' Mrs. Evans had been stood still for a while now and the walking stick was starting to quiver. Mr. Richards saw this as his cue to leave.

'Thank you, Mrs. Evans, although I am sure the walk will do me good, and in this sunshine, I don't mind.' He waved and started to walk away from her.

'Here, Mr. Richards, I don't suppose you've heard any more about this canal talk?' she shouted as he briskly moved away. Mr. Richards hadn't appeared to have heard that final question. Without looking over his shoulder, he made a wave gesture and kept up the pace of his walk. Mrs. Evans sat herself back down in the chair with a large sigh.

Chapter Eight

Margaret braved going into Neath alone. Usually on her way, she bumped into another maid, like Rosie, or occasionally as she was putting on her shoes, David would sign that he'd like to join her. Company also gave Margaret an extra spring in her step and this time, it was lost.

The door slammed shut behind her without her needing to pull it. She jumped. It was only then that the sharp wind went through her body and her bonnet was trying to fall off her head. She tightened the bow underneath her chin even tighter and clung to the blanket in her basket. Not only would this be a lonely walk, but it would also be a cold one, too. The wind stung her nose as she raced to get to the bottom of the hill away from Gellia.

Once past the church, the wind seemed to calm. But Margaret couldn't shake the feeling that someone was behind her. No, she was safe here, wasn't she? Every few steps she turned, but saw no one, nothing. In fact, all the usual people she would see on the walk couldn't be seen anywhere. Where was everyone? Even Coombe Lodge looked like it was unoccupied. No, can't be.

Her pace quickened. She knew the shortcuts now so could dart about and not get lost anymore, like she did in those early days. A large gust of wind nearly blew her off her feet and she stumbled back a few paces. Why did she have to go into Neath today of all days? As she steadied herself, she heard her name.

'Margaret. Margaret!'

She spun round and saw no one. Must keep walking.

'Margaret, Margaret!'

'Who is this? Where are you?' she shouted into the air.

The basket rocked in Margaret's arm, and she started to run. Would she ever be free?

She ran around the corner, then after a few moments of hearing nothing, leant against the stone tunnel.

'You all right, Miss?'

Mr. Tennant.

'Yes, thank you, sir. The wind, it gave me a chill that's all.'

'Take my handkerchief, it may help warm up that face; why, you look nearly blue.'

'Thank you again, sir, you are very kind.'

He nodded his head and walked on. Somehow, she felt safer. Only a few steps away from the butcher's now. Hopefully, the wind on the way back would carry her home.

Chapter Nine

Neath Fair, September 1821

September always signified Neath Fair. A new energy came upon the village with the fair coming - new opportunities, different customers, and in line with the September harvest, a new beginning. Everyone rushed and became much busier than their usual pace. Margaret thought she'd even spotted cranky Mrs. Evans with a spring in her step - most unusual. Mr. Richards had promised all his staff one afternoon off to visit the fair and make the most of the annual entertainment. Margaret, who had recently become more acquainted with Rosie, another maid in a nearby house, had decided that they would go together one Friday afternoon to embrace the atmosphere.

Everyone had told Margaret what to expect at Neath Fair, but they always ended with the comment that until she had experienced herself, she'd have no idea. Every time she heard that, a pit of stomach queasiness wouldn't shift for the rest of the day.

The smell of meat cooking in the open air made Margaret's stomach rumble immediately. There was so much shouting, with sellers approaching the women in the street. This wasn't for her. She thought how peaceful Gellia Farm was in contrast to this chaos.

'Fancy the latest trend here, ma'am?' 'I'll do a deal

here for you, ma'am'. One of the gentlemen, if she could call him that, even winked at her. She had heard accents she'd never heard before.

Rosie said, 'Oh, these gentlemen are from London,' as one passed over a rose to her and she smelt it before wafting it in Margaret's face. She turned her back on Rosie.

'Rosie. You can't accept flowers from strangers,' she said. Rosie took no notice and skipped down the street clutching the rose like it was a precious gem. Margaret had stopped walking, to absorb the atmosphere. This was bigger than Neath market. Probably twice the size.

Out of the corner of her eye, Margaret thought she recognised someone from her old village for a split second – no - it couldn't be. She shivered and ran as fast as her legs would carry her to catch up with Rosie, not wanting to be alone in this busy place. Once caught up, she stood up straight and checked her nearby surroundings. Margaret took a deep breath, dusted down her dress and stood tall. Today would not be spoilt.

'Margaret, Margaret, let's get our fortune told.' Rosie was rushing through the stalls, dragging Margaret who was lagging slightly behind her, and struggling to keep up.

'No, no,' Margaret hesitated, 'what would Reverend Isaac say? It goes against my religion.' She shook her head. Rosie grabbed her arm again as she stopped outside a tented stall.

'Loosen up, moody Margaret! It's a bit of fun – are you scared?' Rosie teased her. Margaret could not help but smile at that.

'Oh, all right, what's the worst that can happen?' They paid their money and headed in.

The room was dark, nearly pitch black, except for one candle that flickered in the corner of the room. Margaret accidentally bumped into Rosie and they giggled.

'Think this is funny, do you?' a voice boomed out of the gloomy darkness. The ladies jumped.

'No, not at all Mrs… Mrs. Fortune Teller.' Rosie replied, trying and failing to regain her composure.

'I'm Mystic Mildred to you,' the voice replied. The ladies still could only see shadows until the cards were passed to Margaret.

'Shuffle, then think of a question and pass the cards back to me when they are done.'

Margaret shuffled the deck. She pondered her question, and eventually settled on – will I find love in St. Catwg? She passed the deck back. Margaret drummed her fingers on the table. Her feet tapped the floor with nervousness. There was a pause. Margaret looked to Rosie for comfort but did not receive any.

'Strength is your past card. You took control of your own destiny by coming here. You had strength, courage, destiny.' Mystic Mildred's words were dramatically spoken with the last syllable lingering for a few seconds. Rosie interrupted her.

'Is that true, Margaret, did you leave Carmarthenshire for a reason?'

Mystic Mildred hushed Rosie and she did as she was told. Margaret remained silent.

'The lovers is your present card. You will fall in love, or a relationship will develop. You may even have two suitors and need to make a choice.' Mystic Mildred's tone softened with this one, much to everyone's relief.

Rosie again got carried away and burst into rhyme.

'Margaret and Llewellyn together forever, until death do us part….'

'SILENCE' was shouted across the table followed by a hard bang on the table. Again, both girls jumped.

'One chance left, Rosie, or I'll be sending you on your way.' Mystic Mildred was firm.

'How does she know my name?' Rosie whispered to Margaret. Another bang on the table was followed by Rosie realising she needed to be quiet now. Mystic Mildred laid out the final card.

'The Moon.' She paused. 'This is a warning card, dear Margaret, you need to tread carefully indeed. Remain alert at all times, and do not always follow your heart. Trust your intuition and do not let feelings get in the way. I wish you the best, and that you stay safe from harm. Take this.' She handed something to Margaret and clenched the girl's fist around the gift so she couldn't tell what it was in the dark conditions. Mystic Mildred left the room and there was an eerie silence. The candle burnt out. Rosie broke the silence.

'Well, after that I don't think I want my fortune read, thank you very much. Would it have been that difficult to say, *Margaret you'll get married and have three children with someone you truly love.* Lovers card, yes, but the Moon. No, no. Unacceptable. Warning? You are the warmest, kindest lady I know, Margaret. Who could want you to come to harm? There is no one in the world that would want to do that to you. No one in the world.'

Rosie kept babbling but Margaret, forcing a smile, thought back to what the lady had said. She couldn't shake off an uneasy feeling. When alone, she opened her fist and unravelled a chain with a locket attached. She didn't mention it to anyone else or ask Rosie as she felt silly for not understanding what it was. She patted it as it hung loosely around her neck.

David had been at the Fair that same day and saw Margaret in the street, staring at something closely in her hands. Respecting her privacy, he had kept his distance but similarly, he felt protective over her due to the thought and care she had given him since her arrival to the farm. Observant, as his eyes were relied upon, he thought she looked troubled and had also noticed the establishment that she had vacated. Rosie was a bad influence, he knew that much. But he'd try and keep a watchful eye on Margaret wherever he could, in case.

Chapter Ten

St. Catwg Graveyard, September 2021

Sam Honey prided himself on his guided tours. The murder stone featured in both of his ghost and local tours. Well known, and well respected, he had an excellent reputation, and the tours were regularly sold out, with booking required weeks in advance.

On this particular day, he was on a local interest tour, and it was a cold, autumn evening in the St. Catwg graveyard. Sam was wrapped up warmly in a dark blue woollen scarf and matching coat that went all the way down to his feet. His thick dark hair swayed with the frigid breeze; his side parting making it look all the more top heavy. He had a captive audience of around fifty people of all ages from ten upwards. Sam knew that if he had children in the audience, he couldn't make his stories too spooky but had to try and keep it light and fun. They all gathered around the gravestone. As he looked up, he saw Angharad, Tommy's mum, who he knew from school. She'd never shown an interest in any local history before, and he wasn't sure they'd ever exchanged words in the playground when picking up the boys. What had brought her here today? His thoughts were interrupted by two children, a boy and girl who had barged past him to measure themselves up against the stone to test their height (an unusual method to check if you've grown, he thought). Both were ever so slightly taller than the stone and felt great power and maturity in being so tall. They then had a debate between who was the tallest. The girl's bun, which sat right at the top of her head, edged her a win by millimetres in this contest. She stuck out her tongue, and the boy chased her around the stone. As he could tell, the children were getting restless, so he cleared his throat and declared,

'We'll make a start'.

It was so cold, his breath could be seen in the night air. Sam watched the parents try and settle the children as they were ushered back to form a family group and made to stand quietly and listen to Sam's next instalment. Both children still bent forward to pull a face at the other child and were wriggling throughout. Sam tried to not let it distract him.

He began. 'A lot has been said over the years about this stone, some true, lots false and much unknown. Feast your eyes on the graveyard, take a good look. Does anyone notice anything unusual?' he asked. The interested audience murmured, discussed with their friends and family and lots of whispers of the word murder could be heard escaping their mouths. No one spoke up. The murmurs hushed and Sam was delighted for the big reveal. 'Look around. All the other gravestones face down towards the church, but Margaret faces out towards the hills. She's the opposite direction to all the other stones.' Sam paused for his audience to take in this new information. There were gasps of astonishment, oh and yes, remarks and nods of approval at this fact. Sam loved this part of the tour best.

'And now for the juicy bit. Why is that? Well. Although the landscape has changed now, you can see where these trees are now, up that hill. That is Gellia Farm where Margaret lived as a milkmaid, and the farmer's son who lived there was the culprit - or so they thought. The local village community wanted to taunt him about Margaret's death by making the stone face his bedroom window, a reminder of his actions. It is said he didn't last in the village long after that and escaped to America or Canada, as he couldn't face the daily accusations.'

'Was he innocent then, Sam?' a member of the crowd asked.

'That's for me to know, and you to find out shortly.' Sam replied, tapping his nose. He continued. 'The other thing worth mentioning here is that there have been many reports over these two hundred years that people have seen the victim walking along the pathway where she was found, and that she walks in the graveyard … as a ghost.' He paused for dramatic effect.

The little girl shouted, 'Ghost!' and waved her arms up above her head circling through the crowd. Her father was unimpressed,

'Cassandra, Cassie, get back here now!'

She waved her arms in front of his face and seeing her father's stern look, stopped and slumped her shoulders to face Sam and listen to Margaret's story.

Sam continued. 'They say she floats up and down the footpath and follows walkers along the route. Most local villagers have seen her in the clothes in which she died, with marks around her neck, holding her basket containing the sheep's head that she'd bought in Neath that same evening. Has anyone spotted her this evening?' A couple jumped and darted around, seeing nothing but the dark, cold air around them. The crowd stood on guard waiting for Margaret to appear in front of them. She did not.

Sam carried on with his rehearsed speech. It must have been delivered at least five hundred times, but it didn't matter to him. New audiences were wowed and delighted with their newfound knowledge and each time felt like the first time he'd ever said those words aloud. Sam was a St. Catwg boy, born and bred, who was permanently fascinated by the murder stone story. The passion took over his life as he spoke to everyone he possibly could to learn more about it, he read every book, found every newspaper article and church record in existence. He distinguished fact from fiction, myth from reality and rumour from truth. Proud to be called the murder stone expert, out of everything he did during his tours, the thing he enjoyed most was taking centre stage at the murder stone itself and telling the ghost story. Sam longed to see Margaret's ghost and always hoped she'd appear, but she never did. He felt like the only person in the village who hadn't caught a glimpse of this alleged ghost.

This tour was coming to a close. 'I'll tell you her full story when we head back to Neath where I'll talk to you about the Mackworths, the Tennants, the Richards's, oh, and I cannot leave out beloved Mrs. Evans, whose ghost will beat me with her walking stick until I tell her story; actually, it's probably her ghost that haunts this graveyard.'

A hand raised. Sam indicated for the man to speak.

'You've got a lot of this wrong you know. You are a fraud.'

The group stopped and stared at the speaker. Whispers broke out. An elderly gentleman had been quiet listening to Sam, not acknowledging the other tour participants and lingering at the back so he was not noticed. He had watched Sam give his talks over the years, listened to his podcasts, read his local history books and even got one of the books signed by him once. But when he poured over the details of one of Sam's stories, he noticed a rather large error and that made him distrust the so-called historian. So, back he went to fact check everything Sam had ever written. Story by story, he noticed names were wrong, dates were wrong; Sam didn't have a clue, only lazy research and a loud voice had kept him going this far.

Today, the speaker decided, no more. Conscious of all the eyes on him, he realised that he must get out of his trance and speak up. He had waited months for this moment to out the smug loudmouth, Sam Honey.

'You think you know it all, but I've done better

research than you.' He held up one of Sam's books with red ink marking splattered over the paragraphs to show the errors. Someone with a torch directed it at the scribblings for the group to see. The gasps and murmurs continued as the old man could see Sam cowering away from the crowd, saying nothing. The group waited.

'I… I... I'm sorry, this tour is now over. Thanks for your time.' Before anyone could challenge Sam, he had bolted out the graveyard and disappeared fast into the distance. The old man smirked. The plan had worked.

'Now let me tell you the truth behind the murder stone. My name is Andrew Tennant,' the old man continued, rubbing his hands together.

Sam stood on some marshland and took some deep breaths. He spotted Angharad in her trademark pink wellies bounding down the hill to catch up with him. Or was she there for a different reason?

'Hi. Who the hell was that guy?' Angharad said.

'Don't know, but he's clearly out to ruin my livelihood.' Sam sat on the grass and started pulling it out the ground.

Angharad sat beside him. 'Everyone knows that you are the murder stone expert. That's why I came to you.'

He looked at her.

'I didn't know you knew who I was.'

'How could I forget you – Sam, Sam the history man?' She gave him a playful elbow and nearly knocked Sam over.

'You remember me from school?' his eyes widened.

'Of course, you presented nearly every week in assembly, I had no choice.'

Sam stopped pulling at the grass and sat still. Angharad zipped up her coat, got up and started to walk back up the hill.

'Wait.'

'What?' Angharad turned back.

'What made you come to my talk tonight?'

'Tommy won't stop saying the word *murder* now he can read the stone and it always terrified me, so I wanted to try and overcome the fear, and I thought who better than Sam, Sam the –'

'Okay, I don't need another reminder of that nickname, thanks.'

Angharad blushed. 'Sorry.'

'Did you get what you were looking for?'

'In what way? Angharad asked.

'Are you still scared?

'I'm even worse, no thanks to you, now I know there's a bloody ghost!'

Sam laughed, which in turn made Angharad laugh.

'Fancy a drink at the Crown?'

He'd spent years of wanting Angharad, he wasn't going to miss his moment. He was glad that Angharad's eyes lit up mischievously.

'Sure. Tommy's at his dads for a few nights, so I have nothing to rush home for.'

'Great! Come on, then, Angharad Wellington

My career may be in tatters after tonight, and your nerves seem to be too, so let's get wasted!'

'Deal!'

Chapter Eleven

Coombe Lodge, September 1821

Mr. Tennant was telling everyone who was prepared to listen that he needed staff for his lucrative canal project. This was now being funded by himself solely, and he hoped the recruitment would be a good news story for the area. Not only had he asked everyone he knew to share it, but he'd also put an advertisement in the local newspaper and popped a notice up in The Crown Inn. There was to be an open day at Coombe Lodge today for anyone interested. He had no idea how many would arrive but hoped it would be popular as this would take a couple years to build and longer-term employment in the area was currently rare.

A small room was opened up in his house to conduct interviews. Coombe Lodge was always immaculate, and he was proud of his legacy and the future of the Lodge. The room today had rarely been used before, so Alice and the housekeeper cleaned it in readiness and tidied it to perfection. A portrait of the newly crowned King George the fourth had been moved into this room specifically for the day. Mr. Tennant was not an obvious Royalist but acknowledged that it felt fitting to show this type of thing to prospective employees in his exciting business adventure. It was intended to show grandeur, but also strong leadership. This room was also adorned with a few ornaments, but like most Georgian rooms, had a false door on the opposite side to the actual door, purely for symmetry purposes. Alice always forgot this and had tried to walk through the false door a few times, never managing to make it through to the other side.

Mr. Tennant sat at his desk and shuffled a few papers. The blank page staring back at him would be filled with names by the end of the day, he just knew it. Voices outside could be heard as a low noise inside the house, and he hoped that meant that there was a queue. Alice swung her head round the door, her fair hair falling loose and her cheeks red.

'Sir, there's a few outside and they are getting impatient now, can I let the first one in?' She smiled.

Mr. Tennant looked up. 'Tidy yourself up, please, Alice; we want to show we have standards here. Then you may let the first one in.'

Alice ran off to the housekeeper who would help her look presentable. Once smartened up, she peered around the front door. The first gentleman in the queue she knew she hadn't seen before.

He was devastatingly tall, with an impressive physique, and a brown mop of hair. He stood, straight backed and serious as Alice approached him.

'Mr. Tennant will see you now. Can I take your name, please?' It was a rare occasion that a man attracted Alice's attention, but this one definitely did. She swooned as he replied.

'Thank you, miss. I'm Jack Griffiths. Can I have your name, please?' He looked directly at her, and she watched him watch her, taking in her blonde locks, rosy cheeks and shy demeanour. Alice blushed.

'I'm just Alice, Mr. Griffiths.' She shrugged, her cheeks reddening further.

'Just Alice, call me Jack.' He took her gloved hand and kissed it lightly. She rolled her head back.

'Let's get you a job, Jack.' Alice turned on her feet to scuttle indoors. It was a relief not to be facing him now as she could try and contain her excitement and get back to the task in hand. Butterflies in her stomach danced and they wouldn't stop. Alice spun round and she watched Jack stare in awe at the interior design of the Lodge. She was used to this reaction when someone came here for the first time and enjoyed seeing their face. The hallway was packed with furniture and ornaments, an elaborate coloured patterned floor, as far as the eye could see. Jack tried to look composed, but his mouth twitched, almost falling open in admiration. Alice knocked at a door about halfway down the corridor.

'Enter.' A stern sounding voice emerged from the other side of the door.

'Sir, first gentleman, a Mr. Jack Griffiths.' Alice half curtseyed, left the room and shut the door behind her.

She took a moment on the other side of the door to appreciate how handsome Jack was. She looked up at the ceiling and bit her lip in delight. Alice hoped he would be employed.

On the other side of the door Mr. Tennant was checking Jack's suitability. He certainly looked presentable but looks could be deceiving.

'Take a seat, Jack.' He pointed towards the only other seat in the room.

'Thank you, sir, and may I take this opportunity to say what a lovely home you have.' Jack swaggered in his seat.

'Ah, thank you, Coombe Lodge is a favourite place of mine.' He studied Jack carefully. 'I say, I don't think I've seen you around these parts before?'

Jack appeared calm, but Mr. Tennant saw through the bluster and observed Jack's fingers tapping nervously against his thighs. 'Ah, you would be right, I've not long left Cardiff, sir.'

'Left Cardiff, you say? That's most unusual. People usually leave here for Cardiff not the other way round. Got some skeletons in the closet have you, Jack?' Mr. Tennant tittered. Jack laughed in response.

'No sir, my latest job fell through and I heard someone from the village talk about the canal, so I thought I would offer my services. I have worked on lots of labouring plots, and this sounds particularly exciting, and long term compared to some other jobs.'

Out of nowhere came a loud crash, and the shriek of the housekeeper. Both men stood up in alarm and as Mr. Tennant went to see what had caused the crash, Alice ran past the door, hoisting up her dress shouting.

'I'm coming, I'm coming, I'm coming!' Both men looked at each other, frowned and decided to continue their conversation.

Alice arrived in the kitchen to find the housekeeper on the floor with a large pile of smashed plates surrounding her.

'Why, what has got into you today?' Alice asked.

'My nerves, Alice, oh, my nerves.' The housekeeper was shaking.

'What's shaken you?' she asked again.

'This canal talk, it makes me nervous. Why, the other day, and completely by accident of course, I heard Mr. Tennant discussing it. I have no faith he knows what he's doing.' The housekeeper stayed sat in her own tears with cracked plates surrounding her. Alice was quick to sweep it all up brushing around her, whilst trying to calm the housekeeper down.

'Oh, Mr. Tennant does know what he is doing, do not worry about that. Anyway, we're employed and he's a good man so let's not distrust his judgement.' Alice reassured the housekeeper who, by now, had stood up and brushed off the remaining plate shards from her person.

'You are right, Alice, of course you are.' The housekeeper dried her eyes and shook herself, trying to pull herself together. The women worked to recover the damage at pace, and it appeared Mr.

Tennant was leaving them to it as he did not join them.

The men, confident that the smash was being swiftly dealt with, and not hearing anymore repercussions, chatted further about Jack's previous employments and Mr. Tennant warmed to him. His mind was made up.

'I say, Jack, I think you will be an excellent asset to this canal project and would like to welcome you on board. I also think that judging by your past experience, you may be better suited to being a bit of a leader. How would you feel to have say, three or four men to manage and you could have a project manager type role?'

Jack sighed in relief. 'This is better than any expectations I had. Thank you, sir, I won't let you down.'

'I know you won't. Now tell me, do you have accommodation for this evening? You are welcome to stay at Coombe Lodge for a couple of nights, if that's useful. I'm afraid you cannot stay longer than a week though.'

'I've been staying at the Castle Inn in Neath, sir, not the warmest place, so would appreciate your offer, if, you are sure?'

'That's settled then. I'll get my staff to set you up a room for a week. After that, I'm sure you won't have any problem finding alternative accommodation.' The men stood up and shook hands.

'Thank you, Mr. Tennant, I appreciate your

generosity.'

'We will talk further once I have engaged some further labour.'

Mr. Tennant rang his bell. Alice appeared.

'Alice, please show Mr. Griffiths out and ask the housekeeper to set up a room as he'll be staying a couple of nights. Bring the next gentleman in.' He wrote down Jack's name and placed a giant tick next to it. He was pleased he had a strong start.

'Right away, sir.' Alice escorted Jack out and led him out of Coombe Lodge.

'Congratulations, Jack. I'll see you later probably.'

'Thank you, just Alice.' He wandered off back towards Neath and Alice nearly forgot to let the next man in. When she saw the queue, she shook her head and went back to work. No one had caught her eye like Jack. She would be daydreaming about him for the rest of the day.

'Name, please,' she barked at the next man. She hadn't even listened to his reply and on letting him in had said, 'Your next candidate, Mr. Tennant.' She then made her way to tell the housekeeper to sort Jack's room out.

On and on during the day she called,

'Next!'

Alice let one man in, and Mr. Tennant was surprised that it had taken him until now to see a friendly face. Bryn walked in with his childish grin and Mr. Tennant declared, 'You have a job, Bryn, you know you always will with me.' The two men embraced and were suddenly nattering away. They had been friends since they were children and Bryn travelled a lot, but always came home, and Mr. Tennant always found him employment. He was always himself around Bryn, and Bryn brought out a happy side in Mr. Tennant. There was a room always made up for Bryn and all the staff named it Bryn's room as no one else dare stay there. His best friend had returned. What a positive day so far. Mr. Tennant shouted for his housekeeper, who arrived in an instant.

'Oh Bryn, it's lovely to see you. I'll double check on your room right away.' She hurried off and Mr. Tennant was left with his mouth open; as per usual with his housekeeper. he did not have a chance to actually speak. She was far too efficient to need much instruction from him, and she was beloved for it. It was exactly how he liked his house to run.

Queues of boys and men were still waiting outside and had all started talking, getting to know each other and sizing up the competition. The smaller boys had suddenly learnt posture to look taller; the nervous ones were now more conversational. Everyone had spotted a girl in the queue, who had tried her best to look like a boy, with badly cropped hair and trousers four sizes too big. Employment for women and girls was proving to be tough in these parts of Wales, so it was no surprise that girls were going to such drastic measures and would do anything out of sheer desperation for employment. Staring out of the window at the growing queue and spotting the young women and girls himself, Mr. Tennant sighed and his positivity, just for a moment, evaporated in a flash of understanding.

Chapter Twelve

St. Catwg, 1821

The village of St. Catwg held an annual 'twmpath' to celebrate the end of Neath Fair. Welsh tradition meant that all of the village could gather in a local field and hold a barn dance. No one spoke a word of Welsh in the village, but all used this unusual word to discuss it, mostly to make it sound more glamorous and feel more special. The twmpath was paid for by Mr. Tennant, primarily as an annual thank you to his members of staff. Over the years it seemed that either his staff had multiplied, or they kept telling friends and family who told their friends. This had soon grown into a party for all. Mr. Tennant didn't mind much, as he was trying to think of any way possible to get the other villagers on side with his grand canal plans.

The field was littered with flags, and the women all wore flowers in their hair, ready for the occasion. There was a designated area for those playing instruments and singing - they were glad to take their places.

Margaret was determined to shake off the weird tarot reading she and Rosie had endured a few days ago, and with the whole village excited and gossiping about this event, she was distracted enough to try and forget about the whole affair. Rosie, on this occasion, had actually been bright enough not to question Margaret or raise the subject matter again and Margaret was grateful for this. Margaret had a white flower in her hair and was wearing a white dress. It was borrowed from a girl in the village, who had worn it last year, but Margaret didn't mind, it was delightful to wear something different. She held the dress clasped in her hands and swayed like a little ballerina doll, tall and poised. Eventually, she lowered her arms, not realising how much lining was in the dress and her arms ached after only a few seconds.

Some of the ladies in the village used Coombe Lodge to get ready - again an unusual permission that Mr. Tennant was somewhat relaxed about this year. Particularly surprising when only last year, Mr. Tennant himself was seen pushing a maid out the door who was enjoying a quiet room in his house with the stable boy a bit too much. The incident had not long stopped being talked about, but it was doing the rounds again with the remarks, 'A year ago today…'. Mr. Tennant had clearly overcome the awkward moment to be so generous this year - and with the canals to think about. Margaret gazed in wonder at the size of house, and she and the dress twirled in amazement at this moment. She knew in her heart that tonight would be special and a night she would never forget.

The men were not so keen to get dressed together like the gaggle of girls. Each in their respective homes dressed to impress. Margaret wondered what Llewellyn might be dressed up in tonight. She couldn't imagine him all smartly dressed. She had told him about her new dress, and he said that he couldn't wait to see her in something different. The men, in trying to keep with twmpath tradition, wore flowers on their blazers. Those in couples wore matching flowers. Those not, would often be seen to be matched with those who coincidentally had matching flower colours. Margaret hoped her white flower was the right colour.

Margaret tried to remember every detail that Rosie had relayed to her about last year's evening. The only two noticeably not present at the twmpath were the vicar and Mrs. Evans who remained at home in isolation. Oh no, there were more than enough rumours without that adding to proceedings tonight. Apparently, the vicar saw this as his one true evening off duty as he knew he'd be left alone and whilst he knew Mrs. Evans wouldn't go, she respected his one night off. Margaret giggled as she thought back to Rosie's story about Mrs. Evans. Rumour had it that she tried to watch from the side lines a few years ago but her walking stick got stuck in some mud and as the men (who were a little merry at this point) tried to carry her home, she swore - figuratively speaking - never to set foot in that field again.

Margaret watched the party goers start to make their way to the field, where Mr. Glebe was playing the fiddle and cheers and claps could already be heard. The field filled up in no time at all, and soon more musicians joined and Mr. Jones was singing some old song that no one knew the words to (Mr. Jones included, who made weird vowel sound noises when the words failed him). The dancing and clapping still continued, even in the more inaudible parts.

Looking almost ghost like, Margaret had hoisted up her white dress, as much as etiquette would allow, and was bounding up the hill. Due to the shadows and lighting, she looked like she was hovering off the ground and floating up to the top of the field. Her face beamed across as she caught sight of his flower pinned neatly on the blazer. White. On approach, he bowed, she curtseyed and they laughed.

He didn't look half bad for a farmer's son. She stared at him, desperate to reach into his mind and know if he found her beautiful. They linked arms in line with the dance, and although Margaret's mind was racing, for the first time, her feet didn't show it. They were in synchronisation, step by step they danced, and Margaret felt lots of eyes upon her. Nothing, or no one could spoil this moment. Those on the side lines when the dance finished, all rushed up to Margaret and were quick to compliment her - on her dress and her dancing. Mr. Richards joined these people and whispered something to Llewellyn, then smiled at Margaret.

After five or six dances, Margaret was out of breath so pointed to the edge of the dance area. He took her hand and they went to a quieter spot under a tree to have privacy – well, as much as possible in a field of too many people to count.

'Have you had a nice time tonight, Margaret?' Llewellyn asked.

'The best,' she replied.

'You look beautiful tonight.' Margaret was glad the shadows of the trees hid her blushing yet again.

'Not so bad yourself.' She giggled nervously; her foot twitch had returned.

'Margaret?' he said.

'Yes?' she replied, looking up at him with her big blue eyes.

'Can I kiss you please?' he said in a whisper in her ear.

'You can,' came her soft reply. She stretched up as he leant forward. They kissed nervously to begin with, like school children not knowing what goes where. Margaret stopped, took a breath and kissed him again. This felt right. Margaret's feet were still. They both needed a moment. Margaret kept her eyes on the ground. Llewellyn lifted her chin so she could look up at him again.

'Let's get back. I think you have a dance or two left in you yet, dear Margaret.'

Margaret snuck her handkerchief into Llewellyn's pocket. It had previously been dropped on the ground on arrival to the field, so it had a smudge of mud on it, but she thought he probably wouldn't notice. After hours of practising, her embroidery skills had recently improved, and she had stitched her initials into the fabric. She was quietly proud of this achievement. Nothing was said as they made their way back to the crowd where the dancing was in full flow.

Margaret was in a complete daze and had butterflies in her stomach. Llewellyn was being sociable, talking to some of the gentlemen, so she joined the girls, saying nothing, but thinking everything.

David hated the twmpath. It was a night he'd rather forget. Not wanting to be alone at the farm, but not able to appreciate the music, he felt trapped on a night like tonight. Margaret had gone over to sign a conversation with him, but it felt rushed and he didn't blame her for wanting this night to herself. Keeping his watchful eye, he saw Margaret and Llewellyn creep off together, hand in hand. It was fair to say he liked them both, but not together. After another beer he headed back to the farm alone. Another twmpath over with for another year. He threw his white flower onto the ground on his way out of the field and stomped on it hard. Good riddance.

Chapter Thirteen

Christmas, Gellia Farm 1821

Time flew and the Gellia Farm residents were now looking forward to Christmas. Margaret particularly enjoyed Christmas as the church welcomed the arrival of baby Jesus. Whilst giving birth in a stable definitely did not appeal, having her own baby did. She let her mind wander for a moment before thinking back to Mary, Joseph and little baby Jesus. The village had plenty of festive activities planned and she dreamt what her first Christmas at Gellia Farm would bring.

Gellia Farm decided to host a small house party with close friends and family in the village. Margaret was worried about so many people squeezing into the farmhouse, but Mr. Richards was dismissive to her concerns, so she went along with it. It did feel a bit cramped early on, and Margaret offered to be front of house, so she had a bit more air.

Mr. Richards was busy being deep in conversation with anyone and Margaret hadn't spotted where Llewellyn had got to.

Two maids from the village had arrived, Gwen and her friend, who Margaret didn't recognise. She had never spoken to them before but had seen them at the twmpath and around the village. She greeted them kindly, always keen to make new acquaintances.

'Merry Christmas ladies, welcome to Gellia.' Margaret smiled sweetly. Gwen pushed Margaret out of the way and both of them ignored her greeting. Margaret stood still, eyes wide, with the front door left open.

'Shut the door, Margaret, we'll all catch a chill.' Llewellyn had re-appeared with an air of authority. Margaret slammed the door shut again and stood open mouthed staring the two women who were now all over Llewellyn as the three of them disappeared off to another part of house.

Margaret stayed on door duty a little longer before curiosity got the better of her and she wanted to see what everyone else was doing. By everyone else, she meant Llewellyn. She checked the entire farm except his bedroom. A deep throaty laugh came from the other side of the door. Margaret hissed and stayed well away.

Keen to enjoy the party, she herself got talking to a stable boy from the Mackworth's house. He was handsome and his body well-muscled but the thing Margaret noticed about him, was the largeness of his hands! She found herself with him most of the night before she realised that she didn't even know his name. They were getting closer and closer until she saw Llewellyn kissing Gwen in the corner of the room. Furious, Margaret lunged at the stable boy who was rather startled but did nothing to stop Margaret in her pursuit. The rest of the party took no notice of any of these antics as they were too busy in being merry, laughing and joking in small groups. Margaret stopped for breath and the unnamed stable boy was ready for kissing again. She leaned forward to see what Llewellyn was doing. But Gwen and Llewellyn had disappeared from view. Margaret switched her own attention back to the stable boy.

'Why, what is your name?' she asked.

'Henry,' he told her.

'Oh, handsome Henry. Of course, that suits.' Margaret stroked his hair.

Henry looked at her, smiling in return.

'I've wondered about you ever since you arrived in the village but thought you and the farmer's son were an item, so I was scared to speak to you. I wanted a dance at the twmpath but thought you'd turn me away.' Henry bowed his head.

'No, no, you can talk to me. We are not a couple.' Margaret lifted his head and kissed him on the lips.

'Yes, it looks like him and Gwen soon will be.' Henry replied.

Margaret chose to ignore that hurtful comment and settled down on the window bench for more kisses.

David had sat in the same corner all evening, with no one to have a conversation with as they were all too occupied. Margaret had kept up at least one conversation with him every day, but tonight was Henry's night. Keen to see Llewellyn distracted from Margaret, this pleased David who smiled to himself at how the evening had turned out. That was until she had lunged for that horse lad from down the road. She wouldn't have meant that. He knew that. Gwen had just grabbed Llewellyn. What a night. Sometimes being the observer was an incredibly advantageous position.

It was into the early hours that people started to leave the farm. A few were sleeping at the kitchen table but mostly they dispersed as the sun came up. Margaret had gone to bed alone and wasn't sure if the same could be said for Llewellyn. She got dressed and sat on the bed. Daydreaming, she couldn't stop smiling at how lovely the stable boy had been last night. She remembered his name was Henry. It suited him. She heard a thud followed by a groan. Llewellyn had woken. She stayed in her room not wanting to see him yet. She couldn't face it. Margaret was certain she'd heard a woman's voice say goodbye. Margaret quivered as she remembered more of last night. Gwen.

She set about the cleaning in the kitchen, on her hands and knees scrubbing away at the sticky floor, knowing that Llewellyn would soon be up and about. Mr. Richards looked up from his newspaper, and Margaret realised Llewellyn was in the room. She stopped scrubbing to listen.

'Good night, son?'

Llewellyn replied, 'Father, my head hurts.' Mr. Richards tittered and went back to his newspaper.

She jumped up. 'Hello.'

'Morning.'

Llewellyn kept standing in Margaret's way as she was now sweeping the floor.

'Get out the way, will you!' she screeched.

Llewellyn clutched his head to remind her of his

headache.

She pushed him out of the way.

'What's got into you? Henry not satisfying you?' he retorted.

'Henry was a gentleman which is more than can be said about you.' She stormed off.

He called after her, 'Gwen would never walk out on me.' Margaret marched back at twice the speed of her departure.

'Well. Good for Gwen. If you want a desperate whore, you've found your woman as I won't be the woman sneaking out of your bedroom in the early hours of the morning. I have my religion. I am a respectable woman. She does not. She is not.'

'You hypocrite,' Llewellyn replied. 'There isn't a person who didn't see you wrapped around the stable boy last night.' She went right up to him, her short frame trying to intimidate him. He laughed at her efforts, being broad and tall.

'I did not sleep with Henry, nor is that going to happen.'

He pushed her away. Mr. Richards slammed his paper down on the table.

'I cannot stand listening to you two squabbling any longer. Silent, Margaret. Be Silent.' Margaret did not want to argue with her employer, so slammed the sweeping brush down and stormed back into her bedroom. Once her door was shut, she screamed. Unable to control her temper, she felt infuriated at men telling her what she can and cannot do all the time. Her and Llewellyn clearly did not have something special as she originally hoped. Thoughts wondered back to Henry. Sweet Henry. Margaret had fled her home to escape men and now they were getting wrapped in her thoughts all over again. Enough. She decided that she'd prioritise the cows from now on. At least they didn't answer back.

Margaret spent the next day keeping away from people and stayed with the cows much longer than she normally would. The events of the party had to be forgotten, and she needed the men of this village out of her head, ideally out of her life, but she had to work. Margaret took the cows down to the field earlier than usual, everyone at the farm was still sleeping. Those crisp early mornings were the best as the air felt so fresh; she felt so alive.

After a long day at the cow field, Margaret let herself into the farmhouse quietly but was startled by Llewellyn jumping in front of her when she had barely opened the front door.

'Sorry.' He looked down at her with an adorable look on his face. Her knotted stomach immediately loosened, and she knew in an instant her heart would forgive him, though her head would still take some time to adjust. Margaret walked past him saying absolutely nothing, head held high. Let him stew for a while, she thought, without a backward glance.

David witnessed what looked like an apology towards Margaret but remained unimpressed. It was clear to him that his affections for her would never be returned, but the fact that they could converse with sign language and she gave him attention as a friend was definitely more than enough. No other woman had paid him that same respect and he was grateful. The next few nights passed with Margaret deliberately avoiding Llewellyn and Mr. Richards and she made more of an effort to get to know David. They swapped old family traditions, and Margaret shared how her previous vicar from her hometown always got too drunk for Midnight Mass and how, one year she could not understand why he was still drunk when she had swapped his drink for something non-alcoholic - what a performance, indeed. David laughed with Margaret until his cheeks hurt and both lost souls recognised each other as family as both were without theirs at this festive time.

On New Years Eve, everyone at Gellia Farm decided to stay at the farmhouse. Margaret was a bit sulky about this as she didn't want to feel that she had to stay with Llewellyn and Mr. Richards when the inn would be more sociable. The atmosphere was still tense between Margaret and Llewellyn. They remained civil, but even a fly would sense an atmosphere. The two men sat in their usual worn chairs, drink in hand and discussing New Year's resolutions. Llewellyn's was to get married. Margaret raised her eyebrows but quickly realised she must not react as that was what he wanted, so she continued to play cards with David, unusually saying nothing. As the clock chimed midnight, David leapt and kissed Margaret. She swung back, pushed him away and looked at him. David signed, saying sorry, and ran into his room. Wanting to avoid any further atmosphere in the house, Margaret chased after him, but he refused to come out. She edged his door open, but he slammed it shut. Mr. Richards and Llewellyn were quick to laugh at the situation and found it even funnier with their additional drunken merriment. Their not so loud whispers could be heard as she walked back into the parlour. She chose not to stop and listen to them and went to bed herself. Not the best start to the New Year. What was David thinking? Poor boy.

Chapter Fourteen

St. Catwg Vicarage, January 1822

Keen to shake off the encounter with David and the Gellia Farm residents prying eyes, Margaret focussed on doing something just for her. Her New Year's resolution was going to be a big one this year and heavily reliant on the vicar for support. This was something she'd never dreamed of before, never thought possible, never dared to dream so big, but she wanted it badly.

Reverend Isaac looked happy to see Margaret and invited her in as she stood fidgeting on his doorstep, awaiting to ask this favour of him. She blurted the request out.

'Reverend, I have thought about my New Year's resolution, and I wish to learn to read and write.' The idea lingered in the air before she continued. 'As much as I enjoy your services, I would like to spend time looking at the Bible myself and understanding it. I also miss my parents and would like the opportunity to write to them once in a while and read their letters back. Of course, they cannot read or write either so their vicar would scribe and read for them, but if I were to write to them myself, well, to do it would be a real achievement. I see Mr. Richards and Llewellyn pouring over the accounts and it looks like scribbles on a page to me. I want to know. Please can you help me?' Margaret stopped for breath, as she realised how fast she had spoken without stopping. Her eyes looked pleadingly at the vicar.

He smiled. 'Margaret, it would be my pleasure. Shall we make a start?'

Margaret clapped her hands. 'Oh, thank you, Reverend, lets!'

Reverend Isaac pulled out the chair at his writing desk for Margaret to sit down. The empty page stared up at Margaret. The quill was already sat in the ink, so Reverend Isaac pulled it out. He wrote her name.

'See if you can try and follow the shapes I made.'

Margaret's feet shuffled nervously under the table as she took the quill herself, swirled it in the ink and poised it on the page. Holding the quill felt so unnatural to Margaret, a foreign object awkwardly held between her fingers. Her tongue stuck out as she tried curling her first 'M' on the page. It nearly resembled a shape, but the ink had smudged all down her hand and then smeared on the bottom of the page.

'Oh. This is more difficult than I ever imagined.' Margaret felt defeated already.

'Try again.' Reverend Isaac prompted.

Again, she dabbed the quill in ink and tried to write her name. It already flowed much easier this time, and she was much more satisfied. After a few more goes, she understood how to use the quill.

'Well done, dear Margaret. I'll give you a harder challenge next time; I shall teach you the alphabet and you shall write it down.' Reverend Isaac patted her on the back as she swirled more shapes on the page. She didn't know what she was doing, but holding that quill gave a sense of purpose, control. Margaret had never felt anything like that power before. With her cows, she knew how to command, but not in day-to-day life. Today was a big step, and with Reverend Isaac by her side, she could achieve anything.

Mrs. Evans had noticed Margaret visiting the vicarage in a much more regular occurrence. Whatever that girl was up to, she did not like it. So, Mrs. Evans asked the reverend what Margaret was doing visiting him at the vicarage so often.

'Why, I am teaching her to read and write,' he replied coolly.

'Read and write? Read and write? She's getting too big for her boots, that girl. It's not a woman's place to read and write, Reverend, she should be here to serve the men of the village.' Mrs. Evans spat out her words and walked off, muttering to herself, not prepared to give the Reverend any more of her time.

A couple of hours later, it was time for the women of St. Catwg to visit the village well. Catwg's Well was built by St. Catwg (Cadoc) who also built the church near the well as it was once the only source of water into the village. The well took its water source from a stream known as Nant Gwladys – after Cadoc's mother. Visiting the well was no longer simply a pilgrimage, it had become a social occasion for the women to have a catch up and gossip amongst friends. Most women enjoyed this time of day, but it was here that gave Margaret the feeling of being an outsider. Mrs. Evans was deep in conversation with Gwen when Margaret arrived. They looked over at her, laughed and then put their backs to her. Rosie and Alice joined Margaret which made Margaret feel more at ease, but she struggled to understand Mrs. Evans' hatred towards her.

Out of nowhere, Mrs. Evans shouted, 'Imagine thinking yourself worthy enough to hold a quill in a man's world.' The women laughed in unison and Margaret hung her head. Rosie and Alice had picked up on the conversation and Alice whispered to Margaret.

'Are you learning to write?'

Margaret nodded her head shyly, 'And read, Alice, yes.'

Alice was impressed. 'Good for you Margaret, can you teach me when you know how?'

Rosie piped up, 'And me.'

'Yes, ladies, of course I will.' Margaret smiled for the first time since she'd spotted Mrs. Evans, who was now scowling at her from across the group gathered around the well.

'Ignore that old lady, Margaret, she's jealous of you and the whole village knows it.' Alice reassured her, patting her on the shoulder.

The ladies said their goodbyes and Margaret made her way back up to Gellia Farm with the water. Perceptions had changed slightly and thinking back to her arrival at the village, Margaret remembered Mr. Richards saying, 'We look after our own.' It was fast becoming a realisation, that maybe she was not one of them and in fact was an outsider, who had to fend for herself. At least she felt safe. Nothing scary had happened for a few months now. The locket still hung tight around her neck, and Margaret curled her fingers around it, praying, hoping for a good year. Today had seemed more positive, and her lessons with Reverend Isaac were going well.

Long may it continue.

Chapter Fifteen

St. Catwg Graveyard, October 2021

Two tall men were stood at Margaret's grave, both in casual clothes, one wearing a bicycle helmet and holding onto a bike. Both were mid-fifties, and clearly not from the village.

'I came to see this stone a few years ago after hearing about it. You see, there is like a rectangle shape within the stone itself, that looks like it's been cut out?' The man wearing a helmet edged forwards to get a closer look at the stone and inspected the rectangle that sat strangely in the middle of the words on the stone. He nodded to the other gentleman, who continued.

'Well, that's apparently where the murder weapon is kept. She was stabbed, see, slit her throat right across her neck, he did, and as a tribute to her with this stone, they hid the knife in the stone itself, so it'd never be forgotten or used again.' He stopped and looked at his friend, expecting praise for such knowledge on the stone.

'Wow, that's amazing, isn't it? So, the knife she was cut with is sitting in that stone? Unbelievable. Thanks for sharing, Tony, that's an incredible story.'

The friend looked genuinely interested in this revelation. The two men stayed chatting at the stone for about an hour or more, as Tony pointed in the direction of all the key story points.

'Murder down there, murderer here,' said Tony, in a voice that was loud enough to echo through the quiet, still graveyard. His friend continued to absorb every word, soaking the information up like a large, soapy sponge.

A couple holding hands walked past as the men were talking.

'Are you interested in the stone?' asked the man, releasing his hand from his partners.

'Yes, my mate Tony here was just telling me all about it.'

'Yes, I couldn't help but overhear. I'm the chief historian to the area,' the man said, loftily.

'Oh?'

'Yes, I'm afraid you've listened to the rumours and not the facts. Here's my business card, feel free to come join one of my tours and I'll tell you the true story.'

'Sam Honey?'

'Yes, and this is my partner Angharad. Seriously come along, both of you, you might learn a thing or two. Or even see a ghost!' Sam took the woman's hand again and they continued their walk through the graveyard, leaving the men staring at a business card. Sam was confident, cocky almost. But he did sound like a professional. Ghost talk, though, how silly.

Later that day, after Tony and his bicycle friend had long gone, Susie went by and placed a rose at Margaret's grave. She did this on the thirteenth of every month for as long as she could remember in memory of that fateful day in July, two hundred years ago, when Margaret was murdered. A passerby came over to her and asked her the story of this stone. Susie, an always excitable storyteller went into elaborate detail about Margaret, how she'd been strangled, and the village response.

Then she quipped, 'Of course, everyone thinks this remained unsolved, but we do know otherwise, you see, it's not widely known.' Excited, she winked at her one audience member and edged closer towards him. Then, she lowered her voice into an almost whisper.

'You see, there was this man, Parry, he was known as, and Parry had a huge crush on Margaret and when she turned him down a few times, he went crazy. Years later, on his death bed he gave a full confession of strangling her in a jealous rage.' Susie backed away from the startled gentleman. He thanked her for the information and then headed into the local pub for a pint of bitter, muttering to himself as he trailed off to The Crown Inn.

Susie said a few words to Margaret (the village already thought she was a little bit bonkers, so no one ever questioned this) and then said goodbye. Satisfied, she went home, feeling like she'd done a good deed for the day. Then she thought back to that lovely gentleman she had been talking to. Susie had definitely not seen him around here before, and he can't be local if he didn't know about the stone. He was well dressed for a Wednesday afternoon, especially around these parts. She wondered what he did for a living, to be dressed like that in the middle of the week.

From the corner of her eye, she spotted Sam and his new love, Angharad, walking past her window. That man thought he knew everything about Margaret and the stone, and yet it sounds like Sam got caught out the other day at the graveyard. How amusing. She was fed up of Sam lording it over this village as the historical know it all.

Conscious of time, she checked her watch and realised it was time for her favourite TV game show. Susie correctly answered the five-hundred-pound question and was now rubbing her hands in anticipation of the one-thousand-pound question.

Chapter Sixteen

St. Catwg, February 1822

With Christmas over and January's freezing temperatures giving way to a milder February, the village settled back into its usual rhythm.

Mr. Richards had asked Margaret to run some errands for the farm in Neath. Margaret was always keen to obey her employer, although she felt a pang of sadness that the day would not be spent with the cows. On her way out of the village, she bumped into Henry, the stable boy who she had forgotten about since the party as they had not seen each other since. A smile flashed on Margaret's face as she walked over to speak with him.

'Hello Henry, lovely day.'

'Is it?' Henry had not even bothered to look up and continued to brush the horse that had accompanied him. Margaret was quick to read her audience.

'Why, Henry, have I done something to offend you?' Margaret blinked quickly as she waited for a response.

Henry shrugged. 'You tell me, or better still, talk to Llewellyn about it. He's yours now, isn't he?'

Margaret was taken aback at such a grumpy reply, she found it sweet that Henry might be jealous but had not expected such a strong reaction.

'Oh, well, I'm not sure what we are.'

Margaret looked down. She did not want to talk

about the matter further.

'Well, if you are happy being second best, Margaret, good luck to you. I wouldn't use you like he is, though. Start using your eyes and ears. Why do you think you've been sent to Neath today? Llewellyn is with Gwen and they want you out of the way. Why do you think he's late home every night? He's at the Glebe's house.' Henry spat on the floor.

Margaret replied, 'He is not. They haven't. I never had you down as a jealous man Henry, I am incredibly disappointed in you.' A strong breeze whirled between them, and Margaret steadied herself to keep her bonnet on her head as the wind tried to snatch it from her. Too engrossed in his horse, Henry had paid no attention to her or her bonnet. Why couldn't he even look at her?

Margaret stamped her foot and forced out an indescribable noise whilst scrunching her hands into fists. 'Good day to you, Henry.'

'I'll wait for your apology when you see I've told the truth,' he called after her, then shook his head and continued to brush his horse. Margaret turned away. She wouldn't give that lad a second more of her attention. As if he knew anything about Llewellyn.

David had been for a quick walk when he saw Margaret and Henry in what looked like a heated discussion. Lip reading was not David's forte, but he endeavoured to try and follow the conversation. 'Llewellyn' was recognised immediately but not much else. Margaret definitely looked tense after that conversation. Luckily for him, her facial expressions and gestures meant he could read her well, even when she was not signing for him. Today, Margaret was not a happy woman.

Still feeling embarrassment from his New Year's Eve actions, he wanted to prove to Margaret that he was serious about her. It was also clear she needed cheering up, which was most unlike her. With Valentine's Day around the corner, he saw this as the perfect opportunity. David was incredibly skilful with his hands and knew that Margaret never entered the workshop, so he set to making her a Welsh love spoon. This was a small gesture, that much he knew, but still he wanted to show her how much he cared. He thought back to other designs he had seen previously and decided that flower and bird designs would be the most appropriate for her as she loved nature. Hours were spent in between his farm work on this wooden creation, and he hid it in the barn so that no one else would know about it. The night before Valentine's Day, it was complete and David was satisfied with his work. Still feeling awkward after her rejection on New Year's Eve, he decided to creep into Margaret's bedroom before she got in from bringing the cows back to the farm and place it on her pillow. The plan was set.

Margaret came home and had completely forgotten that it was Valentine's Day. Like she had promised to herself, particularly after New Year, she was directing her attention to the cows. They didn't let her down. Work done for the day, she entered the farmhouse, kicked off her shoes and lay on her bed for a moment. When she moved her head, she realised that something hard was underneath it. Margaret spun round to see a beautifully carved wooden love spoon on her pillow. Her fingers curled around it, claiming it as hers. She clutched it in her hands and pulled it into her chest. This was the most wondrous gift she had ever received. The detailing was divine. Margaret jumped off the bed and raced around the farmhouse to find Llewellyn to thank him, but she could not find him. It was then she realised that he must have snuck home after she'd left that morning so that he could surprise her. With the gift still in her hand she brushed past David, not stopping to speak or acknowledge him. Realising that Llewellyn was nowhere to be found, she sunk into the chair in the parlour and admired her gift even more. She stared at Llewellyn's creation over and over, twirling it in her hand like it was a graceful ballerina meant to be spun.

A couple of hours later, Llewellyn arrived home. The smell of alcohol appeared to be on his clothes and his breath as soon as he entered the farm. Margaret ran up to him.

'Thank you for my Valentine's Day gift.' A kiss was placed on Llewellyn's lips and Margaret chose to ignore the alcohol fumes pouring off him. Mr. Richards was in the kitchen and peered his head round the corner to stare at Margaret. She ignored him.

'What?' Llewellyn almost choked.

Mr. Richards interrupted before Llewellyn drunkenly said something stupid and upset Margaret all over again.

'What did Llewellyn get you, Margaret?' he asked.

'It is not what he got, it's what he made. Look.' Margaret held up the spoon. She watched their reactions as Llewellyn smiled his lovely smile at her, Mr. Richards sported some kind of frown, and David looked sorrowful as he hung his head. What was with these men? Smug, confused, jealous? She didn't need this. Llewellyn had given a declaration of love whether they liked it, or not.

Mr. Richards patted Llewellyn on the shoulder. 'Well done, son.'

'Thank you, Father,' came the not so sober reply.

Any doubts about Henry's words earlier in the day had now dissipated into a distant memory. Llewellyn loved Margaret. The spoon told her so. Henry knew nothing, she knew everything.

Chapter Seventeen

St. Catwg Church, March 1822

The church looked increasingly like it was going to collapse or cause serious injury or harm to a parishioner. The struts holding the church up looked less sturdy, and rubble occasionally fell to the ground off the crumbling structure. The largest place of worship in the area, it was always full to the brim with people on Sundays, with the congregation having travelled far and wide to hear Reverend Isaac. This side of the river remained passionate and loyal to the faith through Reverend Isaac's powerful sermons and empathetic responses.

An emergency meeting had to be held to discuss the future of the church. It had to be deliberated whether it was to stay, and money sought for urgent repairs, or if it was actually not salvageable and it was time to pull it down. Villagers, and those from surrounding areas, were nervous about how this may go and it was clear that there would be a high attendance rate at this meeting.

Despite being elderly, and being able to soon settle into retirement easily, Reverend Isaac did not want the church to be torn down. Not because of his job, but for the people of St. Catwg and beyond. It was more than a place of worship, but a place of community, where people came together, in birth, marriage and death, where new beginnings started, and where support to those in need could be ministered. It was of his view, that every village needed a church, and they were needed more than ever, rather than to dispose of them. Whilst he acknowledged that his views may be old fashioned, he knew the church was much needed. It was time to air his views.

The day of the meeting arrived, and it was led by Mr. Tennant, as a leading member of the Parish Council. Feeling somewhat guilty over his funds being used on his own business venture and therefore not in a current position to fund the church repairs in their entirety at the same time, he felt somewhat awkward about the whole thing, but it was his duty to chair the meeting and in that, Mr. Tennant would not fail. The hall was full, and with only a couple of chairs left unoccupied (recognising the likes of Mrs. Evans would not be able to stand for such a long time) more people edged into any gap they could in order to hear what Mr. Tennant had to say and the ensuing debate. The local newspaper reporters had covered the story so far and placed themselves around the edge of the room in order to hear the latest instalment. They hoped they might be able to influence the decision if more people knew and hoped to pressurise those who could afford it, to contribute to save the church. The hall was babbling with noise as everyone gossiped while they waited for the meeting to begin.

'Thank you all for coming on such an important

matter. I have been asked to gather and collect your views which the Parish Council will then consider before making their final judgement. I will be taking notes and trying to ensure that as many people as possible get their views heard. Of course, we cannot be here all night, so if I cut you short, please accept this early apology. The strength of feeling matters to us all and this is a difficult problem. Whilst I suspect most of us want the church to be kept, a solution is required as to how this might be funded. Current quotes suggest an amount of two thousand pounds is required, so I would like to hear your solutions if you have any, as well as your viewpoints. I'm going to start by asking you to raise your hand if you wish the church to be repaired and maintained.'

A large show of hands reached into the air and Mr. Tennant gave nothing away as he nodded to this response.

'Those who think the church should be knocked down?' Some hands were in the air, but it was clear how few shared this view, compared to the church being maintained.

'Thank you. I can see we may have a difference of views in the room. All that is left for me to say is, lets please remain respectful to everyone's views at all times. Who wants to start us off?'

Hands swarmed up and Mr. Tennant pointed towards Mr. Drummond to speak.

'I think it's time for the church to go. We are a modern Wales, and those that want to remain attending church can do so in surrounding areas. I am worried that it's a dangerous place, and the repairs are far too costly and lengthy for it to be worth saving.'

Mr. Tennant scribbled down these thoughts and heard that there were some murmurs of agreement amongst the group. This was not the start he was expecting. More people followed Mr. Drummond's line of thinking, and Mr. Tennant was left worried that maybe the church would not be saved after all.

Mr. Tennant noticed that Mrs. Evans was unusually quiet, although as he thought back to their previous conversation, he recalled she had said she'd remain quiet as the youngsters may have a better way of getting their views across. But he didn't think for a second she'd actually remain this quiet. Still, the night was young.

Mr. Tennant was trying to interject the next rambling man who wanted the church knocked down but was being ignored. His hand tapped the table, but still the man continued.

Suddenly, Margaret shrieked. Mr. Tennant sat with his mouth wide open. The entire hall stopped and stared at her. Mr. Tennant saw Mrs. Evans roll her eyes. Maybe she would speak up after all. Whilst Mr. Tennant was grateful the last man had stopped talking – after this outburst the man had no choice, but he was interested in what this woman might have to say.

'Mr. Tennant, may I speak?'

Margaret tried to compose herself as she stood up.

'Well, you've certainly now got all of our attention, Miss…?'

'Margaret Williams, sir. Milkmaid at Gellia Farm.' She smiled at him and he indicated for her to proceed.

'Why, I have only been in this village for less than a year. But part of my work involves walking past our crumbling church every single day, but every day I see something wonderful happen. People meeting, praying, visiting loved ones, and much more. When I first arrived in St. Catwg, I saw immediately that this church was the heart of this village and to knock it down, would destroy that heartbeat for the villagers. Our congregation, we know, is wider than this village - so this does not just affect St. Catwg, but further afield. I am forever grateful to Mr. Richards, the family, and the village as to how welcome I have felt. I never imagined this to be possible living away from my home, but I have made this place my home now and I believe that the church had a significant role in this feeling. Mr. Tennant, I know you asked for solutions, and I'm sorry I'm not business like enough to help there. But the amount of money that you quoted sounds too high to me. I cannot help but feel that only the essential work should be done at this time, and I cannot help but think that this may reduce that price. Mr. Tennant, maybe that is where you could help us and our church? I will fight for this church. I hope to get married there one day, have my child baptised and I pray that is not too much to ask for. Thank you.'

Margaret gave a curt nod and stared down at the floor once she had finished. The hall erupted into applause and comments of support were said to Margaret. Mr. Tennant sat and just stared at her, feeling the change of atmosphere in the room she had caused. Even Mrs. Evans stood up, applauded, then when meeting Margaret's eye, nodded. Mr. Tennant looked over at Mrs. Evans as he'd seen this exchange and raised his eyebrows at her. She turned her head away from him and sat back down promptly. He must continue to chair this meeting somehow, although it did feel like Margaret had saved the church.

'Thank you, Margaret. Anyone else?' Mr. Tennant asked.

'Yes, just to say, that whilst I have tried to stay quiet, as I am sure everyone knows which side I am on as it were, I have to say that this church *is* at the heart of this community. Margaret is absolutely right. I hope to see more of you there, particularly if you are cynical, as I would like to try and change your mind. Thank you and thank you, Margaret.' Reverend Issac smiled.

Margaret beamed at him and her smile lit the room.

'Thank you Reverend, does anyone else wish to speak?' Mr Tennant led the conversation once more, but the hall was silent, and people shook their heads. He realised in that instant why Margaret was so readily accepted in the village, by most anyway. What a bright young woman, maybe she'd be bored of being a milkmaid and could come and work for him. She had a great future if she was given a chance.

'Very well. Thank you, everyone. I will write this up and it will be considered by the Parish Council. Then they can make their judgement. Margaret, I am happy to take forward your suggestion and see if I can reduce the quote. Meeting ends.' Mr. Tennant shuffled his notes together, tucked the chair behind the desk and set off back to Coombe Lodge. He heard Margaret's name on everyone's lips as they departed the hall.

The Parish Council read and discussed Mr. Tennant's proposal and agreed to save the church with the reduced quote for essential works only. Mr. Tennant had added in his notes, 'I believe we have a Miss M. Williams to thank for this.'

Chapter Eighteen

St. Catwg, January 2022

Comments came in about the Murder Stone at an alarming rate in the St. Catwg visitor book. What soon became apparent, was that it wasn't visitors commenting, it was the local residents, from their own village. *'It's creepy,' 'It's haunting us,' 'I swear it casts a shadow and moves; I think she lurks!' 'Enough!'*

The residents of St. Catwg found the murder stone abhorrent and intolerable. Even though two hundred years had passed, the word 'Murder' chiselled on the gravestone, haunted and provoked the villagers. It still had the same effect it had on Mr. Tennant, all those years ago.

One parishioner, a particularly well-known loudmouth in the village, impinged on Reverend Maurice. Not one to expect an invite, Mrs. Irons waltzed into the vicarage unannounced and caught Reverend Maurice munching at his lunch of sardines with bread and a large dollop of butter.

'Do come in, Mrs. Irons,' he scoffed between mouthfuls. His cheeks were full, like a hamsters, and the hairs from his moustache bristled as he spoke.

'I've had enough of her staring at me!' Mrs. Irons screeched and then looked disgusted towards Reverend Maurice who was adjusting his napkin down his front to take another chunk of his sardines. It was a rather large portion, and he was taking enormous bites. Once finished this particular mouthful, he dabbed his mouth and spoke to an impatient Mrs. Irons. For a vicar, he was disgusting.

'Who?' He looked around aimlessly. This did not help matters.

'Her. The murder stone girl. The stone stares at my house all hours, every day and night. I need your support to help me get the stone removed. Now!' Mrs. Irons was talking faster the more she spoke and was almost breathless by the time she finished.

Reverend Maurice was unhelpfully dismissive. 'I'm sorry, but you know I cannot influence graveyard affairs. You saw what happened last time. I agree there should be restrictions on what can be written on gravestones, but I have no influence, Mrs. Irons. You'll need to take this up with the Parish Council.'

Mrs. Irons flew up her arms before leaving the vicarage without saying another word. Useless man. How dare the Reverend refuse her request! This murder stone needed to be taken down, forever more.

The Parish Council gathered every first Wednesday evening of the month in the local village hall and were about to discuss a strongly worded letter from Mrs. Irons, about the murder stone. It read,

'Dear Parish Council members,

I write to you with great concern over this murder stone.

The murder happened around two hundred years ago, everyone involved has been dead for a long time. This is a respectable village and one that has passion, integrity and love for its parishioners. It is a disgrace and unimaginable that the murder stone should be haunting this village for even a second longer. It is unacceptable, and I would like to propose to the council that it is removed, and St. Catwg moves on. It might be our history, but it is not our future.

I have included the signatures of other residents who agree with me that the stone must be removed. I trust that this will give you the sense that I am not alone in this endeavour.

Please confirm to me that you agree and provide the plan to remove this vile stone in its totality.

Your Sincerely,

Mrs. Irons'

The council members stayed silent, thinking about this request. Sam was ready to protest, but just as he opened his mouth, Mr. Gronow broke the silence.

'We can't do that; it's a part of the village history!' He was adamant in his response.

'You don't live anywhere near it, though; I can imagine that it is a bit creepy in the dark when you are drawing the curtains,' Mr. Adams replied, shuddering.

The council of twelve started talking at the same time, with no one argument particularly being heard or acknowledged. Sam needed this to be a conclusive result.

As chairman of the council, Sam watched as the animated gentlemen showed no sign of stopping. He crinkled his face before shouting,

'Enough, enough! I can see that this has divided opinion so I do not think that we can ignore Mrs. Irons' request. Those of us that know Mrs. Irons, also know that she will not let this rest until some action is taken.'

Murmurs were heard in agreement from around the table.

Sam continued. 'I propose that we provide a high railing fence around the graveyard. That should block out any immediate viewing of the stone, particularly from that row of houses from which we have received the complaint. However, as Mr. Gronow says, the murder stone is a part of this village's history, I believe that it should remain in its rightful place and the victim should have had justice.' More nods and sounds of approval came from the table; but Sam knew there was more to say.

'This is an integral part of the village, and we still get visitors due to its local importance. The church still needs donations, and the stone contributes hugely to that. My tours wouldn't be the same without it. We need this stone. Margaret's ghost would never rest without it.'

Sam was mostly ignored and had noticed the eye rolls round the table as he was talking. He decided to move on, thinking enough had been done.

'All those in favour of a high railing fence and the Murder Stone to remain say Aye!'

Sam was resolute and knew that no one would dare go against this proposal.

He was right, as all twelve hands lifted in the air

and 'Aye' bellowed across the room.

'Unanimous decision, gentleman, excellent. I'll write to Mrs. Irons immediately.'

Mrs. Irons was surprised to see such a quick response from the council as she expected more push back. However, their proposal met everyone's needs. She ran in the house to tell her husband, who raised one eyebrow.

'What have you been meddling with now?' He looked apprehensive.

'Nothing, look.' She handed him the letter. He read it closely and nodded.

'Well done, darling. An excellent result. Proud of you.' Mr. Irons kissed his wife's forehead and marched up to bed. She hugged the letter as she was grateful that the village had supported her, she was often challenging, but this time she had won.

Chapter Nineteen

Gellia Farm, April 1822

The shock news that Mr. Richards had to travel to Cardiff, so would be staying overnight rippled through Gellia Farm. Whilst both Margaret and Llewellyn acknowledged the event but appeared dismissive, the minute Mr. Richards left the room, they rushed towards each other to quietly make plans for that evening. Margaret was biting her nails.

'I'll treat the other staff to some money at the Crown and we'll be alone.' Llewellyn spoke with authority.

Margaret's face turned pale and she looked wide eyed.

'If that's what you want,' he added, as an afterthought. They kissed and she slowly nodded. Llewellyn was tapping his foot in his large boot, and the noise was making Margaret anxious. Her religion did not permit any sex before marriage, but Margaret shook her head at the thought that Llewellyn would suggest that anyway. He was a kind-hearted gentleman - wasn't he?

Mr. Richards left Gellia Farm that April afternoon and with the bribery of money for the inn from Llewellyn, the staff trundled off down the hill. David slammed the door behind him, giving one last glance to the couple. Margaret and Llewellyn were alone, and Llewellyn didn't anticipate spending the time downstairs. As the footsteps of the rest of the staff receded into the distance, he said to Margaret, 'Come.' So, she followed him upstairs, where they cuddled in his small bed and she held him tight.

'Margaret?' he said.

'Yes, Llewellyn?' she replied.

'You know I want you to be my wife one day?' he said, calmly.

'You do?' she squeaked.

'I can't propose to you yet as I'm saving up, but as soon as I have enough money, I'll tell Father and we'll marry as soon as I can. If you want to?'

'Yes, yes of course I do.' Before she properly finished what she was saying, he grabbed her for a kiss.

They stood up to slowly undress. Margaret knew. Her heart overruled her head. She wasn't thinking about God, or her religion, or anything else in the world in that single moment. Just Llewellyn. They stared at each other naked. Margaret fidgeted with excitement and anxiety, so Llewellyn lifted her up and laid her back on the bed.

'Are you sure you are comfortable with this, future wife?'

Margaret nodded. 'Yes, I am my most wonderful, handsomest, lovely, did I say handsome already, oh, I think I did actually, hang on a minute…'

'Margaret.' He stopped her. 'Please do not spoil this moment with so many words.'

She kissed him and he kissed her everywhere before entering her slowly.

'Please, now talk Margaret, are you feeling all right?'

'Yes, I'm good.'

'Are you sure?' he asked.

'Yes, Llewellyn.'

He was passionate and tender and she was relaxed, so glad to finally be feeling wanted and loved. Feeling conflicted, she was mad at herself for waiting to do this for so long but also recognised that she wouldn't have wanted this intimacy with any other man. Both of them were wrapped around each other in passion and urgency. Llewellyn cried out and Margaret gasped. He laid on top of her for a moment before slowly pulling out and kissing her. She was now a woman. It felt strange. They lay side by side and Llewellyn nudged her chin to come closer to him. He looked deep into her eyes.

'Are you sure that was all right, and you are all right?'

'Yes, yes, oh! Llewellyn, I love you so much,' she whispered, trying to catch her breath.

'I love you too, dear Margaret, my Margaret.'

A few hours into the night they heard the others come in drunkenly from the inn. Llewellyn continued to hold Margaret. They were ignoring everyone and everything else. This was just about them. Margaret had never been more sure of anything in her whole life.

'Stay here until morning,' he murmured.

His voice was persuasive and Margaret couldn't think of any reason why she should want to leave.

They woke the next morning and smiled, remembering the night before.

'My future wife,' Llewellyn said.

'It wasn't a dream.' Margaret replied.

The others were still sound asleep, and Mr. Richards wasn't due home until later in the day. They kissed and Margaret tip toed into her own room. The moments kept replaying from the night before over and over in her head. Llewellyn was the gentlest gentleman she had ever known, she thought, wrapped up in an idyll of love for him.

Later that day, Mr. Richards returned and declared, 'I may have some more regular business in Cardiff for us, Llewellyn, so I'll be travelling up there and staying overnight there more frequently in the future.'

Llewellyn acknowledged this with a simple, 'Yes, Father.' Margaret couldn't look at him in that moment, but when Mr. Richards left the room, they whispered to each other.

'Did you hear that?' Llewellyn said.

'Yes, I did, what excellent news and timing.' Margaret said feeling a little flush.

'Father? When you next going to Cardiff?' Llewellyn asked, with a grin. There came no reply.

David was making his way into Neath with a list of things to get for the farm. This was a task he hated as he had to solely rely on people's good nature to work out that he was deaf and to support him. It always felt that the same people that helped him previously were never around a second time to help him as before and he had to try and explain his situation, and what he needed. On the way, he bumped into Margaret's friend, Rosie. who appeared to be on the same journey as him.

Upon seeing David, Rosie signed, 'Hello, D.'

David could not believe that Rosie had just signed to speak to him. Yet another moment of the brilliance of Margaret; he had no idea that she had taught Rosie some basic sign language, and yet here was her friend, signing to him. It had to have been Margaret, as no-one else would have bothered. His world had got a little bit bigger as he had someone new to converse with. David's heart panged when he realised, he loved Margaret even more than he thought humanly possible. But Rosie had also wanted to sign, too, what an honour. She reaffirmed his thinking.

'M Teacher' Rosie told him.

David clapped and smiled at Rosie's efforts. Rosie still had plenty to learn so finger spelt out the word 'h-e-l-p' to David. He nodded and the two of them walked into Neath. Rosie was showing David on their route that she could now spell the whole alphabet in sign language. It was clear that David could not have been happier to have someone new to talk to, his body language had altered. Rosie used sign for 'Again' so David knew to go slower and repeat whilst Rosie was learning. Both parties were patient with one another, realising the difference that this would make to both of them. The dreaded journey into Neath and around Neath had now rejuvenated David once more, all thanks to Margaret.

Chapter Twenty

Coombe Lodge, April 1822

It was all go-go-go at Coombe Lodge. There was a new buzz about the place as the Tennant Canal was commencing construction. Mr. Tennant had spoken to his team at length over the past few weeks about the plans, the land and where to start this work. Everything was running to plan, except one thing. This required Mr. Bullins to give up a small section of his land, and as it stood, he was refusing to change his mind and agree. Mr. Tennant had sent him a strongly worded letter last week which had received no reply. Pacing up and down his drawing room, pondering on how to tackle this problem, Mr. Tennant rung the bell for his housekeeper's assistance. Out of nowhere, she arrived in an instant.

'Ah. Keep; I require your assistance.' Mr. Tennant used the jocular name he had given his housekeeper many years ago, to be used only when the two of them were alone and mainly for his own amusement. 'How well do you know Mr. Bullins?' His elbow nudged her in a teasing manner.

'Oh, well, umm, not that well, sir, we are not that well acquainted to be honest with you, sir.' Keep stared at him like she had just swallowed a wasp.

'Quiet, Keep. I do not mean like that!' Mr. Tennant was hasty to respond to his housekeeper's disapproving look. 'I mean, have you noticed his favourite clothing, does he have a favourite food or drink, a tipple, does he carry something strange with him as he walks or talks?'

Mr. Tennant's pace grew more rapid, as if he was chasing a dog on a lead that was getting away from him. Keep shook her head at all the suggestions. Mr. Tennant sighed when suddenly, Keep looked up as if having a grand idea and closed the drawing room door, so that no one else could hear what she had to say, primarily Alice.

Keep held her voice at a whisper.

'You know sir, that day where you wanted to tell the gentlemen about the plans for the canal, that first day, there was an incident.'

Mr. Tennant boomed, 'Incident?'

Keep shushed him and they both sat down on chairs facing each other. Unable to stop working, the cushions were plumped up for them both first before taking their seats.

Keep told Mr. Tennant exactly what had happened between Mr. Bullins and Alice that day, and how he had behaved inappropriately towards her. Mr. Tennant gave a sharp nod at Keep's information and immediately stood up, asking for his coat and hat. These were swiftly brought and Mr. Tennant marched out of the door without saying another word.

On arrival to Mr. Bullins's house, Mr. Tennant had prepared exactly what he was going to say to that man. A loud knock followed and a maid opened the door. 'Poor thing,' Mr. Tennant muttered, before marching straight in and past the maid, who remained stood at the door with an open mouth.

'Mr. Bullins.' Mr. Tennant was firm.

Mr. Bullins pulled down the newspaper from in front of his face, shook it and slammed it down next to him.

'I do not remember inviting you here,' he said, folding his arms.

'You did not reply to my letter,' Mr. Tennant stated.

'Busy,' Mr. Bullins muttered and pulled up the newspaper, back to where it previously was, directly in front of his eyes.

Mr. Tennant by now had had enough and proceeded to pull the paper down so he could see the ignorant man and speak with him.

'You are giving me that piece of land or I'll ruin your reputation by telling everyone what you did to Alice,' raged Mr. Tennant.

'Who?' Mr. Bullins had a giant smirk on his face, which Mr. Tennant needed to wipe off in an instant.

'My maid.' Mr. Tennant's temper was being tested.

'Oh, that slight young thing!' Mr. Bullins smiled.

'Well, she bent over, asking for it she was, I was only trying to help.' Mr. Bullins went to lift up his paper again.

'Maid, maid!' Mr. Tennant called. The same small, ginger girl who had opened the door to him, now appeared in the doorway.

Her face was pale and she kept her head down.

'What's your name, please?' asked Mr. Tennant, inviting her into this awkward conversation.

'Florence, sir.'

'Now, look here, Tennant,' shouted Mr. Bullins, but Mr. Tennant continued, neither concerned nor troubled by any posturing by the so-called gentleman.

'Do not worry about Mr. Bullins, Florence, but tell me, has this man ever touched or groped you inappropriately?'

Florence's lips started to quiver but she said nothing. The look in her eyes revealed everything Mr. Tennant had been told about Alice. It must have been happening to this young slip of a girl here, too. Suddenly, Florence began to sob, and Mr Tennant pulled out a chair for her to sit. Mr Bullins was outraged.

'How dare you enter my home unannounced, accuse me of assault, then question and upset my maid. She's not allowed to sit in here.'

'I'm sorry Florence. Truly, I am. Bullins, you are giving me that land before I share this news with everyone to ensure you neither touch another maid again nor have any good reputation to speak of. Florence, please pack your things, you are now employed at Coombe Lodge, with more money than you are getting now.'

Florence ran up the stairs as fast as she could and Mr. Tennant said a final few words to Mr. Bullins who had lost his voice in the drama.

'I expect the deeds to your land to be sent to me within the next two days, or I will act.' Mr. Tennant left the drawing room and waited for Florence in the hallway. It took only seconds for Florence to pack and rush to leave with her new employer. Mr. Tennant was impressed with how swift she had been to gather her things and leave. She'd do well at Coombe Lodge.

A few days later, a thick brown sealed envelope arrived at Coombe Lodge. Mr. Tennant had received the deeds, alongside a scrawled, unsigned handwritten note.

'You are a plague.'

Chapter Twenty-One

Gellia Farm, May 1822

He had never been in love before. Llewellyn wasn't entirely sure that this *was* love. How were you meant to know? When he saw her that first evening, tired but still so happy and content, his whole world lit up. It was clear that he had been existing up until that point. Weeks went by and he tried to ignore the feelings he had. Conscious not to make things awkward at the farm, he wasn't sure his father would approve of the match. Llewellyn also wasn't sure if she had any feelings for him. He couldn't tell. She was so warm and friendly to everyone she met, that in no way did he feel singled out or special. How, aged in her twenties, had she not been married yet? That question replayed in his mind, over and over. Gwendolyn Richards. It certainly had a ring to it indeed.

Llewellyn, however, decided to continue his dalliance with Margaret and visited her at the cow field as much as possible during the daytime, and found any excuse to speak to her in the evening. There seemed to be this way about her which made him want to tell her about every thought in his mind. Llewellyn had always been such a private person prior to meeting her, but for some reason, he felt safe talking to her. His father used to ask him question after question in the hope that he would eventually speak up, but only basic answers were ever given, certainly no conversation starters. Thoughts raced back to his mother, who he missed dreadfully, as she had died when Llewellyn was only a small boy. However, somehow, he knew that the feelings he had for Margaret were not of the romantic kind. The love he felt for Margaret was different to the love he felt for Gwendolyn, although he continued to have Margaret entertain him in bed, he did not want to share his life with her.

Margaret woke up and realised she felt different somehow. After being sick a couple of times, and realising how she constantly felt queasy, it dawned on her that she hadn't had her monthly cycle, in, well, more than a month, almost two! A baby. Out of wedlock. The shame. But the excitement! They had to get married soon. She sat on her bed for a moment and held her stomach. She was finally getting everything she had ever dreamed of. A good job, a lovely home, a husband, a baby. She couldn't wait to tell Llewellyn and banged on his bedroom door to tell him the news. He wasn't there, so, still in her nightdress, she looked for him in the kitchen. There he stood, tall and handsome as he had ever looked.

'I'm pregnant.' Blinking, her eyes were wet with happy tears, it felt strange to say this out loud. She went to give him a cuddle. Llewellyn said nothing but gently pushed her away, holding her by the shoulders and stepping away. It was not a violent gesture, but in that single moment, Margaret knew that this was not going to be the single most happy moment of her life to date. Llewellyn's head dropped to the floor, and he could not look at her.

'I don't want this,' he mumbled.

'What? What are you saying?' Tears were already falling.

'No. I don't want this. I didn't ask for this. I think you might need to leave.' He spoke up slightly louder this time. She kneeled on the floor clutching her stomach in tears. Mr. Richards walked in.

'What's this?' Mr. Richards said. Neither Margaret nor Llewellyn spoke for a while.

He asked again. 'What's this?'

Margaret gave him the courtesy of replying. 'I'm pregnant sir, Llewellyn's the father. I thought he'd be happy, but he does not want me.'

Silence overtook the room. Llewellyn finally spoke.

'She's lying, Father, I don't know who she's been with, but it's not me. I'm no father.' Margaret took a large gasp at the lies spiralling out of her lover's mouth. She couldn't say all the things that she wanted to say so remained on the floor making loud noises between the sobs.

Mr. Richards looked at them both. His eyes penetrated this woman on his floor. Margaret had never felt so alone, and betrayed. How could Llewellyn lie to his father in that unemotional way? Where was that tender, loving man who had promised her marriage? She couldn't breathe.

'Cardiff, sir. You were in Cardiff. He sent the staff away, he promised marriage. You have to believe me. You have to!' The words were becoming desperate out of Margaret's mouth. Mr. Richards had to believe her. He had to. But he continued to stare at her saying nothing. In that moment she knew he'd choose his son over her. After all, blood was thicker than a pregnant milkmaid. Her thoughts were soon reaffirmed.

'Margaret. I am terminating your contract immediately and I'm sorry but by tomorrow morning I need you out. Llewellyn, I want you to think about your behaviour, but I recommend that the two of you do not converse any longer.'

Margaret leapt up off the floor and wiped her eyes. 'Oh, don't worry, I'll be gone by tonight. I know when I'm not wanted.'

Her arm brushed against her face to wipe the tears, and she rushed to her room to dress and pick up what few belongings she had. Margaret had no idea where she might go but thought she'd start with the vicarage as the Reverend always knew what to do. She hoped he'd be more forgiving than this family.

'Brute!' she bellowed as she slammed the door at Gellia Farm for the final time. She regretted that she had not said goodbye to David, but she would catch up with him away from that place and those people.

Margaret struggled with her suitcase but was determined to make a quick getaway. Her forever home was not meant to be as she thought. In a matter of months, her dream was shattered. She'd got it wrong again. Catastrophically wrong.

Unsteady on her feet, she took her time to walk down the hill towards the vicarage. Whilst she had more possessions leaving than she had on her arrival, she clung to her locket hoping that it would give her courage, and luck. She needed luck. Margaret already knew that Mrs. Evans would spot her by the vicarage with a suitcase. Curtains would soon twitch and she would be the talk of St. Catwg, like she probably was in Llangyndeyrn, but hadn't stuck around to find out. Luckily, the village was quiet. Margaret made a conscious decision not to look towards Mrs. Evans' house as she'd be lurking at any moment. She knocked on the vicarage door. Reverend Isaac took one look at Margaret, and she saw his face drop. He was so intuitive. Margaret couldn't stop shaking. What if he turned her away? He had every right to. She'd have to go home. Then she'd be even more at risk.

'Come on in, Margaret,' said Reverend Isaac and he led the way to the sitting room.

Margaret sank in his armchair and sobbed. He seemed to catch the odd word between her breaths.

'Llewellyn... baby... so mad.'

Reverend Isaac encouraged her to calm down. 'Breathe Margaret, breathe, whatever has happened here, it will be all right and I'll support you.'

He gave her a warm smile as he went to make them a cup of tea.

Margaret looked troubled and then said, 'But Reverend, I have sinned.' She sobbed again. He passed her a handkerchief out of his jacket, and she smothered it over her face.

'Llewellyn promised marriage. He did. I would have never… I would have never…'

She was hysterical at this point whilst the reverend caught up. Nodding in all the right places, he said nothing and she was thankful for it. He showed her up the stairs to his bedroom. Why was she in his bedroom? She collapsed on the bed too quickly to give it a second thought.

'Rest, Margaret, rest.'

She curled up in a ball and closed her eyes, still wet with her tears.

Reverend Isaac was having an uncomfortable night's sleep on his sofa that evening, but he didn't mind. His parishioners always came first. He must tidy the other bedrooms. He'd been saying this for months but never got round to it. They were full of books scattered all over the floor, or his notes. It would take a good few days to tidy up. Besides, he'd never had a visitor before. An hour later, he checked on Margaret and she was sound asleep holding her stomach. He did not know how this would resolve itself, but he hoped Mr. Richards would see sense and Llewellyn would become honest. Margaret certainly did not seem the type of woman to sleep around, plus she was mostly loyal to her religion.

Reverend Isaac suspected that Mr. Richards knew the truth as much as he did, but family first. Margaret didn't deserve that treatment. Thinking back, he remembered that he'd never asked what had exactly happened with the previous milkmaid who had also left Gellia Farm abruptly. He hoped that this wasn't history repeating itself. The difference there was that the previous milkmaid hadn't immersed herself in the village as Margaret had been so successful doing. She must have left unnoticed. Reverend Isaac vowed to visit Mr. Richards in the morning. Hopefully then he and his son would have calmed down, and Margaret could maybe even marry Llewellyn. Reverend Isaac felt protective over Margaret and had often thought about what it would be like to be officiate at her marriage.

Reverend Isaac's thoughts slowed down as he sat in his armchair. He dreamed of Margaret's wedding to Llewellyn. The villagers were dressed in their best outfits. Everyone smiled, as Mr. Richards was the proud father he had longed to be. Only Reverend Isaac, Margaret, Llewellyn and Mr. Richards knew about the baby, so when Baby Richards arrived everyone would think that the baby was slightly early, that's all. There was a thud upstairs which made the Reverend jump. Startled, he was snapped out of his dream and back to the dark reality of Margaret and her baby upstairs. Disorientated, he struggled to get back to sleep after the thud, so checked that Margaret was safe.

She was still sleeping soundly, looking peaceful. It appeared that the thud was one of his leatherbound bibles fallen to the floor. Reverend Isaac slowly, and as quietly as possible, picked it up to place it back on the shelf. It fell open on the page of Proverbs, 28:13 *'Whoever conceals their sins does not prosper, but the one who confesses and renounces them finds mercy.'* He slammed it shut. Margaret sighed and made a stirring noise, so he took the bible with him and crept out the room. Once downstairs, he wanted to go for a walk but didn't want her waking up alone. He sat and prayed for Margaret and her baby, wishing for a positive outcome. Reverend Isaac did not know what else to do. To comfort himself, he tried to read his favourite passages from the bible which previously had always given him comfort in times of drama and conflict. Today, however he could not concentrate on reading anything, so he decided to get up and dressed and do something to resolve Margaret's situation.

Reverend Isaac knew he couldn't have Margaret stay a day longer - he was already risking his reputation by her staying the one night, even in an emergency such as this. He spoke to a few villagers about the sorry situation and wondered if Mr. Jones might like having Margaret around. A more elderly gentleman who could do with the company, perhaps. He knocked on the door, greeted Mr. Jones and the man let him in. Last night's dreadful events were explained. Mr. Jones sat listening and nodding in all the right places. When Reverend Isaac had finished, Mr. Jones sighed and placed his hands on his knees.

He coughed before beginning his little speech.

'I am going to tell you something now that no one knows, Reverend. I am like Margaret's baby.' Reverend Isaac started to mumble something, but Mr. Jones held out his hand as if to silence him.

'Let me explain first, Reverend, if you please. My mother, God rest her soul, was lured by a man, like Llewellyn has Margaret and then she was pregnant and broken hearted. She was so ashamed and worried about people judging her, so moved away and pretended to be widowed. I don't want a young woman on my watch to have to go through the same as my mother. Margaret is also new to the village. I can pay her a small amount until the baby comes for her to run errands for me. It is settled.'

Reverend Isaac listened carefully and nodded. Mr. Jones would look after Margaret, and a working arrangement would be suitable.

'You are a good man, Mr. Jones. I know not many will share the views that we do, and I have to be particularly careful, so I appreciate your values. Sometimes life isn't as clear as we expect and whilst she's been stupid, Llewellyn has been more stupid by not making an honest woman out of her. I am disappointed in them both, in truth. I hope he sees sense. But thank you for supporting Margaret. I'll tell her the good news now.'

They both stood up, shook hands, and Reverend Isaac walked back to the vicarage. He shouted for Margaret on his way through the front door. She appeared with a blotchy face and dark eyes.

'Good morning, Reverend. I'm so sorry to inconvenience you yesterday, that was dreadfully awful of me. I thought Llewellyn would be as happy as me, but his reaction was unexpected. Anyway, I'll look to finding alterative sleeping arrangements right away.'

Reverend Isaac smiled. 'No need, my dear. I've come back from Mr. Jones' who said if you help him in the cottage with household duties, he is happy for you to stay there for the foreseeable future. A small wage will also be paid.'

Margaret took a breath. 'Oh Reverend, thank you, thank you, and what a lovely fellow Mr. Jones is. Oh, I shall enjoy taking care of him.'

It was the best situation he could hope for - for now. He noticed that Margaret was still trembling.

Reverend Isaac decided to distract Margaret. 'Now, what do you say we have another reading and writing lesson before you make your way to Mr. Jones?'

Margaret sprung up to take her place at the writing desk and the two of them settled down to look at letters and shapes. As they sat there, studying and learning, Reverend Isaac was aware that Margaret was still shaking. Her foot kept tap, tap, tapping on the wooden floor, a sure sign of how anxious and wound up she was. More letters formed on the page revealing Margaret's writing progress, which pleased the old vicar. Everything else did not.

Reverend Isaac sighed. It was not for him, or anyone else to judge. Had she done the right thing in coming to this village and getting into this predicament? It suddenly appeared perhaps not.

Part Two

Chapter Twenty-Two

Day 0 – July 1822

The small village of St. Catwg was silent.

Margaret had been into Neath on Mr. Jones' instructions. They needed food for supper. The few weeks she had spent with Mr. Jones had flown by at some speed. She missed her job at the farm, and her cows, and she still missed Llewellyn despite him denying her existence - and that of her unborn baby. Of course it was his. Still, Mr. Jones had been kind taking her in when no one else had. He'd make an excellent grandad of sorts to Baby Richards. She made the point of regularly calling her baby by this name and to anyone who'd listen, purely to spite the family she was so certain she'd be a part of until she was so cruelly rejected.

It had been a busy Saturday for Margaret. To show how grateful she was to Mr. Jones, she constantly tidied, cooked, washed, cleaned and anything else that needed doing. Nothing was too much trouble, and Mr. Jones was enjoying her company. Recently widowed, he recognised that his cottage needed a women's touch and Margaret was the woman for the job. He insisted on helping her lift heavy things - more so in recent weeks, but otherwise she flew around the place, getting everything sorted. They had a similar sense of humour and laughed when she clumsily dropped something, or they noticed Mrs. Evans wearing a new hat to church that didn't suit her scowl. Margaret couldn't stop smiling. It was a great feeling to be a part of this village community and even Reverend Isaac had forgiven her in what felt like an instant for being with child outside of wedlock. He reassured her that she had been wronged by Llewellyn and so the vicar supported her as much as he could.

His support led the rest of the village to follow his lead. Well, except, of course, traditionalist Mrs. Evans who cursed and criticised Margaret at every single possible opportunity. She disagreed with the vicar's approach and whilst she was quick to declare this, her relationship with Reverend Isaac never changed, because, to his face, she was saying exactly what he'd hoped to hear. Margaret rolled her eyes thinking of the old woman's ways. No, without Reverend Isaac's support, she could've been in a tricky position. More than tricky, homeless. Margaret certainly had given her vicar a moral and religious dilemma.

Thank goodness for faith and forgiveness. Mrs. Evans certainly hadn't grasped that concept and Reverend Isaac commented to Margaret and another parishioner that he was surprised Mrs. Evans' walking stick had not actually snapped in two the amount of times she smacked it on the floor in some sort of annoyance because once again, Margaret had won.

Evening came and Margaret had walked into Neath, to collect a sheep's head for supper. Mr.

Jones had fancied one as a treat for dinner that evening and Margaret had fancied the walk despite the wet weather. She placed the sheep's head in her basket, thanked and paid the butcher and made her onward journey back to Mr. Jones'. She giggled to herself as the basket bumped into her bump and she clung to it tightly.

It was raining heavily that day and the ground was wet and muddy, like a thick sludge. Even the air smelt damp. Margaret was treading carefully across the marshland and hoisted up her dress out of the way. The wind made her hat flap around, and she was struggling to balance the basket, hat, and sheep's head all with a belly. She thought she heard a movement behind her, like someone else was also stepping through mud. Slap, slap, slap across the boggy ground, she turned around swiftly. With nothing in sight but trees and the marshland she carried on steadily back to Mr. Jones' house.

Margaret had wanted to stop and rest. She could not believe how tired she was getting at the moment. However, with the howling wind and persistent rain, she decided not to stop. Her pace was much slower than it had been at the start of the walk. She halted to study the ground (as much as she could with her body blocking the vision) and realised she would have to tiptoe in order to make the climb up the hill. Step after step demanded thought and effort. The journey felt endless, so she was glad when the church steeple came into view at the top of the hill.

Out of nowhere, she was grabbed from behind at

the waist. She shrieked. The basket flew out of her hands and started spinning, eventually slowing and stopping a few feet away from her, just out of reach. The sheep's head followed, coming to rest near the basket.

Her assailant had hold of her and was shaking her.

'Margaret.'

She recognised his voice instantly.

He spun her round to face him and held her by the neck, all the while maintaining eye contact. Her stomach was being pressed into his body. She squirmed. Her hat had toppled off her head; her hair blew askew in the wind. Sobbing, she knew this man would be the death of her and her unborn baby.

'Please, please, my baby.' She choked the words through her tears and tried to scream but he placed a hand over her mouth whilst keeping the other tightly around her neck. She could no longer make a sound. Her breathing grew more urgent. He hushed her. The village remained silent. The rain had temporarily stopped. Nothing or no one could be heard. Darkness surrounded her and the baby.

'It's time you were silenced for good,' he told her, as he removed his hand from her mouth and placed it on her neck. Now, he held both his large, strong hands around her delicate neck, tighter and tighter. She tried to fight him, at least at the start, but his rage gave him strength, and she could fight no more. Suddenly, she was being shaken violently. Her head snapped back and forth on her neck, which bore the imprint of his fingers. She tried to protect her baby, but her arms were limp. Her head slumped onto her chest and he stopped shaking her, putting his hands around her neck again. Squeezing and squeezing the life from her and her baby until there was silence. No resistance. No gurgles of terror. No pleading to save her. Just silence.

He grinned. Quick to recover, he looked around and recognising his work was done, he released her and let her drop to the ground. He retrieved her locket as a souvenir for his work. Margaret lay, half her body in a puddle, half out. Her belongings were left as they were, wavering in the wind, the sheep's head staring vacantly at Margaret's dead body.

Mr. Jones looked at the pitch-black outside. It was much later than the time he expected Margaret home and he was worried and concerned. He was not even hungry anymore as his stomach churned so much with panic for Margaret and her baby. Whilst he knew the Richards' family weren't best pleased with the situation, he thought they may come round and persuade Llewellyn to marry Margaret, apologise and let her settle back at their home in Gellia Farm. He opened his front door, but the village was sleeping. He knew he needed to get out and find her, but something stopped him.

Mr. Jones remembered what a chatty and friendly woman Margaret was, smiled to himself, and knew that the silly girl would have got herself wrapped in a conversation and been far too polite to leave. He also knew he couldn't wake anyone else up at this time of night and if there was something wrong, it'd be foolish of him to go out alone. No, he'd call on the reverend first thing in the morning after the service to see if they could find Margaret. He prayed, hoping that she was safe.

Margaret's body lay motionless in the dead of night, alone and bruised. Time stood still for her and her unborn child. Her killer was long gone, and her rescuer far too late. Her long brown hair was matted, and the weather had ruffled up her clothing. She remained half immersed in a deep puddle, unmoving, unflinching. The only witness of this treacherous crime was that of the never eaten slaughtered sheep's head which sat with its eyes fixed on her body. Ever watching and ever knowing the truth.

Chapter Twenty-Three
Day One

Sunday service was about to start, and Mr. Jones kept craning his neck in the hope that Margaret would arrive with the Richards family. He kept shuffling in his seat willing her to come sauntering in with a long-winded story that she may never get to the end of before Reverend Isaac began his service.

As the vicar stood at the chancel ready to commence the service, a clatter of the church door startled the congregation and the Richards family, plus David, sheepishly crept into a pew at the back of the church.

Mr. Jones saw immediately that there was no Margaret to accompany them but did not want to disrupt the entire service unnecessarily in case Margaret had a valid explanation. Throughout the service he turned his head in disbelief that she was not sat with them. Where had she got to? His fingers tapped on the back of the wooden pew in front of him. He hadn't realised how loud it was until people stared in his direction. How stupid he was to have talked himself out of going to look for Margaret. Maybe he should interrupt the service. He stood up, then sat down again, his head glancing in every direction, hoping, praying that he had made a mistake and Margaret was sat right amongst them.

David entered the church and immediately looked for Margaret. He was irritated that they left Gellia Farm late as he always looked forward to his pre-service chat with Margaret. Mr. Jones was sat in his usual seat, David recognised that Margaret was nowhere to be seen. Unaware that the family had already caused a disruption by arriving so late, David tried to get the vicar's attention as the service started. He took it upon himself to stand up and was signing 'M' with three fingers in his left palm. Reverend Isaac had never learnt sign language so had chosen to ignore David's efforts to communicate with him and creased his brow and whatever David was trying to say was lost in misunderstanding. David sat back down with the Richards family who clearly hadn't even noticed that his friend was missing.

Reverend Isaac had been so distracted at delivering his latest service that he had failed to notice Margaret had not attended. In his usual farewell greeting, he was at the door of the church wishing his congregation well, shaking hands and making the usual small talk. He had a slightly longer chat with Mrs. Evans but on seeing that Mr. Jones was pacing backwards and forwards, he decided to hurry her along and see what was troubling Mr. Jones, who was clearly agitated. That was the precise moment he realised Margaret was missing.

'Mr. Jones, is something wrong with Margaret? Why isn't she here? Is the baby all right?' Reverend Isaac asked. Mr. Jones looked at his feet, then winced. He pulled such a face that Reverend Isaac simply could not determine what was the matter with him.

'You, see, um… Reverend, Margaret never came home last night.'

Reverend Isaac's mouth opened and wouldn't seem to shut.

'You mean to tell me she's missing?' he asked.

'Yes, well I guess so, Reverend, yes. She went out to get our supper and never returned.' Mr. Jones couldn't help but stumble on his words.

'And you are choosing to leave it until now to tell me, Mr. Jones?' Reverend Isaac boomed and Mr. Jones looked away, ashamed. He saw Mrs. Evans, who was nearly home, realise there was some sort of conflict and watched her perform a dramatic turn to head back to the church from where she had just come.

'Yes, Reverend. I'm sorry, I thought she'd come through the door this morning, all jolly saying she and Llewellyn had sorted their differences, or whatever these young 'uns say these days, I don't know.' Mr. Jones was still pacing back and forth in the path leading to the church door. Reverend Isaac had his hands on his head and attempted to start a sentence, then stopped again.

Eventually, the reverend said, 'Right, well, we've seen most of the village leave my church without her, so that rules out anyone at Gellia Farm, and, well, like I said, she didn't attend alone or we'd have seen her. She's not with anyone from the village, so it is safe to assume she is missing!' His voice grew shrill as he became more agitated.

'Therefore, we must follow her route back from Neath and ask anyone we bump into if they have seen her.'

Mr. Jones nodded and placed his hand on the other man's back as if offering silent assent. As he turned, he saw Mrs. Evans slouch and change direction again, this time hobbling through her front door and shutting it firmly.

Reverend Isaac and Mr. Jones went around the side of the church and left via the back passageway. They then followed the path along to reach the marshland behind the church. It didn't take long before they saw Margaret laid down in the ditch. They skirted down the hill to reach her as quickly as possible, and drawing level with her body, they recognised immediately that they were far too late. Little had changed since the night before. Margaret was in the same position and her few belongings scattered close by. The sheep's head remained staring at her, now joined by the two gentlemen.

Reverend Isaac crouched down to get a good look at her.

'Oh, Margaret.' He bowed his head.

Mr. Jones let out a massive sob and kept repeating the words, 'I failed her, I failed her.' He couldn't look at her, so had his back turned away from the body. His body shook and he was violently sick.

'Mr. Jones, I'll stay here,' Reverend Isaac took charge. 'You go and find whoever is our volunteer policeman of today and bring him here.' Mr. Jones nodded. 'I think I heard from a parishioner that it might be Stanley's turn this week.'

Mr. Jones nodded again before setting off to find the local policeman.

With Mr. Jones out of the way, Reverend Isaac had a chance to study the scene. No weapon, marks on the neck, but there weren't many other clues. Careful not to move her, he pushed Margaret's hair out of her face. Her bump stood out prominently; he hadn't particularly noticed it before. Reverend Isaac thought of all of the possibilities that had happened. Llewellyn and Mr. Richards were angry with Margaret, but murdering her, if this was what he was staring at? Murder? There were definite signs of a struggle, but he knew that Margaret would never do something to herself. He felt compelled to stand up, to take a deep breath and process the severity of the situation.

Llewellyn could hang.

This had to be murder.

He walked around Margaret, double checking for clues. It was a drier day than yesterday, but she had been stuck out in the rain. With the reverend recognising Stanley was a kind, pleasant young fellow, but that murder was too big for him to handle, Reverend Isaac knew he had to investigate. There would be doubts about the Richards' family's involvement, but he would solve this case and deliver justice for Margaret! After what felt like hours, Reverend Isaac saw Stanley and Mr. Jones bounding down the hill. He wiped his brow forlornly.

'Stanley,' he said. They shook hands. Stanley gasped at the sight of Margaret, putting his hands over his mouth in shock. Reverend Isaac rolled his eyes at the immaturity.

'We'll get justice, Reverend, don't you worry,' Stanley said, patting him on the shoulder. He continued. 'I've arranged for the body to be collected so nothing more needs to be done here. I'll wait and then I'll pay a visit to Gellia Farm. Assuming they were all at church today?' Reverend Isaac nodded, leaving Stanley to it, for now.

He marched up the hill to Gellia Farm. He was grateful to have avoided Mrs. Evans on this occasion, as it would not have been helpful to the village for her to be one of the first to know. The thought that he could not see her also suggested that Mr. Jones hadn't bumped into her either. One small crisis averted.

After the long walk, he reached Gellia Farm and knocked hard on the door. Llewellyn answered.

'Nice to see you so soon again, Reverend. I'll go and get Father, one moment.' Llewellyn turned to find Mr. Richards.

'I need you both, urgently, please, Llewellyn.'

Llewellyn had never heard Reverend Isaac speak with such a sense of urgency in his voice, so found his father as speedily as possible. They both sat down, the reverend remained standing.

'I'm afraid I have some bad news. Margaret's body has been found this morning. It looks suspicious.' He paused, giving the gentlemen time to absorb the news.

'Margaret, no. That was not meant to happen. I had promised to marry her, but I didn't mean it.'

Llewellyn unexpectedly blurted out. Mr. Richards and Reverend Isaac exchanged a shocked look at Llewellyn's outburst.

'What did you say, son?' Mr. Richards enquired.

'I might be the father to Margaret's baby. I might be.' Llewellyn continued to punch anything in his way as he paced up and down the parlour. Mr. Richards and Reverend Isaac edged further away from him.

'Then why did you throw her out the farm?' Reverend Isaac asked. Somehow, he stayed calm.

'I met Gwen and realised my feelings for her, and she's much better than Margaret!' He flailed his arms around uncontrollably.

'This is a mess.' Mr. Richards sent a sideways glance over in Reverend Isaac's direction.

'What do you know so far, Reverend?' Mr. Richards asked crossing his arms.

'Mr. Jones advised me after the service today that Margaret never came home last night after visiting Neath Market. So, we went to retrace her steps but sadly, it didn't take long to find her. She was found in a ditch behind the church.' Revered Isaac looked at the two men, watching their reactions closely.' I'm going to be honest with you. It looks like murder.' He looked directly at Llewellyn when he said the word and then continued.

'Stanley is there now with Mr. Jones, and the body will be collected to determine the cause of death for certain.'

Mr. Richards pressed for more information. 'Why does it look like murder, Reverend?'

Reverend Isaac moved his hands up to his neck but them dropped to his side again.

'She had bruising around her neck.'

There was a long silence where all three men went into their own trance like state before Reverend Isaac realised he was probably intruding.

'Well, I wanted you to hear this from me, before anyone else and I wanted you to hear the facts. I'll leave you to discuss.' He edged towards the door.

'Llewellyn, you were here on your own last night. You didn't leave the farm, did you?' Mr. Richards asked his son. Reverend Isaac froze on the spot, unable to move.

Mr. Richards pressed. 'Llewellyn, answer me quickly, boy, or you could be on a murder charge in a matter of hours,' he shouted in Llewellyn's face.

'Yes, yes! I was here at the farm, Father. No matter what I thought about her, I wouldn't hurt Margaret.' Llewellyn shouted back. Reverend Isaac left Gellia Farm, closing the door firmly shut behind him.

Mr. Richards continued his line of questioning at Llewellyn, not wanting to be caught off-guard again.

'Why didn't you tell me you had committed to marrying her? I would have been happy for you.' Mr. Richards was kicking the ground but only succeeded in scuffing his boots.

'I didn't want to. I wanted her to think I would. I never expected her to become pregnant.'

'But Llewellyn you know how...'

'Yes, Father I know, but I didn't think it would happen so soon.'

Mr. Richards sighed and patted his hand on Llewellyn's shoulder.

'Everyone will think you did this,' Mr. Richards said. He sat down to try and stop his restless body from moving.

'But I didn't. I'm not a murderer.'

'I know you aren't, son. But throwing her out whilst pregnant if you loved her does not look good to a jury. Plus, you were home alone last night.' Mr. Richards had started drumming his fingers on the table, unable to keep still.

'Why are you so sure that I'll get arrested?' Llewellyn looked up.

'There won't be any other suspects. Everyone loved her. Except you, it seems, well, and Mrs. Evans but she's so law abiding and not strong. No-one will suspect her of murder. This is not good. I told the reverend I expected a July wedding with you two,' he said, still drumming his fingers on the tabletop.

'You thought that?'

'Yes, I did actually. I saw your face the day she arrived. You woke up. You looked up for the first time. Your shyness disappeared day by day. I had hope it would be reciprocated.'

'Wouldn't you have cared that she was staff?' Mr. Richards noticed that Llewellyn looked stunned at his father's words.

'No. I wanted you to be happy.'

David saw Reverend Isaac leave, so he signed,

'Where M?' to the Richards men.

Mr. Richards spoke clearly and enunciated the word, 'Died,' back to David, so the boy could lip read. David saw the word form on Mr. Richards' lips and then ran to his room.

Reverend Isaac walked down the hill, pondering Llewellyn's confession. The next few days were about to get complicated indeed. He saw Mrs. Evans outside her cottage.

'Reverend, why has Stanley been here?' she whispered, moving up close to him.

Reverend Isaac sighed. 'I'm afraid Margaret's body was found by Mr. Jones and I after service today.' The words still felt unnatural coming out of his mouth. He thought that he may never get used to it and certainly didn't want to get used to it.

Mrs. Evans stared disbelievingly at the old vicar, her lips moving as though she was speaking but her words were inaudible to Reverend Isaac.

'I beg your pardon?' he asked.

She answered him more appropriately.

'What trouble has that reckless girl got herself into now? Killed herself, I expect.' Mrs. Evans tutted and shook her head.

He stopped her cold.

'Actually, Mrs. Evans, I'm sorry to say it looks like murder, actually.'

Mrs. Evans took in this revelation. 'Well, well, well! I can't say I'm surprised but that is dreadful for this village. A killer on the loose. How terrifying. I tell you what, Reverend, you can't trust anyone these days, except yourself, of course, I will always trust my reverend.'

Reverend Isaac could sort of hear that Mrs. Evans was still wittering on but needed some time alone so had stopped listening. When he looked up, he realised that she had been talking this entire time, so he graciously nodded and smiled in all the right places - or so he hoped.

'Does Llewellyn know?' Mrs. Evans edged closer to the vicar on asking that question. Luckily Reverend Isaac had acknowledged her question enough to process it and respond.

'Yes. I've been to Gellia Farm and delivered the news. You may as well know now, Mrs. Evans, that Margaret had actually agreed to wed Llewellyn. He had asked her. I don't, however, think he meant it.' Mrs. Evans' stayed mouth open with no words coming out. Reverend Isaac thought that this must have been the first time that had happened. She stayed frozen, mouth gaping open. Reverend Isaac coughed.

Mrs. Evans snapped her mouth shut in an instant and muttered. 'Thank you, Reverend,' she managed a smile. 'Excellent service as ever yesterday.' She stumbled back into her house leaning heavily on her walking stick.

Reverend Isaac looked at her in puzzlement, then realised she was trying to block out the horror of a potential murder having been committed. Sighing, he headed back to the vicarage. He needed to be alone. Immediately. Finding Margaret like that would stay with him for the rest of his life.

Chapter Twenty-Four

Day Two - Morning

Stanley had only been in his role for a fortnight; he could not believe his luck that a murder case had fallen into his lap during his first month! Normally, the area of St. Catwg was a sleepy little place. Mr. Drummond, who had been the nominated officer prior to Stanley's arrival, had not been disturbed much, although once when two men in Neath got a little rowdy outside The Railway Inn and one had punched the other with such force that he was lying on the floor unable to move. Mr. Drummond pulled the man up off the floor and took him home to his wife. The man had sobered up quickly on the walk home and did not want the matter pursued. The other man now nicknamed 'Puncher' slurred that the man on the floor had started it and he was just walking home. The matter was not discussed again, although the nicknamed appeared to stick and Mr. Drummond was now gone and Stanley was in charge.

Stanley was going door to door in St. Catwg that morning to see if there were any witnesses to Margaret's murder. Thinking like a policeman, he suspected not, but wanted to try and be thorough in his questioning. However, he also wanted everyone to know it was him taking on such an important case. Stanley looked like he was still a boy of thirteen with a slim figure, dark hair and terribly bumpy skin. This was his chance to prove himself as a man, or so he hoped. Nobody in the village knew if Stanley was his first name or his surname, and Stanley liked this fact because it made him particularly enigmatic. Instinct told him the best place to start, so he began by going to Mrs. Evans' as he knew the village gossip would have something to say. He rapped on her door.

'Good morning, Mrs. Evans,' he said with a degree of formality.

'Oh, hello Stanley. Are you in uniform? Are you the one to solve this murder?' she asked. He felt her eyes on him, staring intently.

'I hope so, Mrs. Evans, any ideas who it might be?' Stanley gave a playful nudge nearly elbowing her in the ribs and then winked. She flinched.

'Stanley, you need to be taking this far more seriously. A nearly innocent young woman has been killed in the God abiding village. I say nearly innocent; silly woman shouldn't have been pregnant with Llewellyn's child but all that's too late now, and you have the cheek to wink at an elderly lady. Do you think a murderer would respond to a wink? Good day to you.' She went to slam her front door, but Stanley had leant forward to keep it propped open.

'Mrs. Evans, I do apologise; I am taking this seriously. I must avoid a terrible crime such as this from happening again.' He stood tall and tried to look as sincere as he could manage, the corner of his mouth twitching at the sides.

'Well, start at the Richards' house, then, Stanley.

At least speak to Llewellyn. Good day.' Mrs. Evans slammed her door with her walking stick this time so Stanley could not jump to reach it. It slammed abruptly in his face.

Stanley, knowing St. Catwg well, swiftly made his way up to Gellia Farm. Not hearing or seeing anyone, he walked around to the farmhouse entrance and knocked on the door, but no one was home. Not willing to give up, he went to try and open the door, but it was locked. He knocked again, only this time louder. There came no reply. A strange noise caught his attention. There was a weird snuffling noise around the back which Stanley wanted to check out, so he crept around the edge of the farmhouse. Muttering to himself, he convinced himself that he wasn't snooping, but doing important police work. The noise got louder, and Stanley thought it sounded like a male grunt. Prepared for conflict, he got out his truncheon from his belt in readiness for what he might find. The wind was whistling through the trees, so there was an additional rustle of leaves and the sound of the breeze, which confused things further. The smell of farming became more pungent, so Stanley held his breath as he was about to turn the corner. He stopped briefly a moment, dazzled by the view. Gellia Farm was so high up, he could look down on the whole village. Even the church and Mrs. Evans' cottage could be seen so clearly from here. What an excellent watching spot. Stanley was interrupted by another loud grunt, and he jumped at the noise. He started to tiptoe towards the noise, which got louder and more frequent. It was getting muddier, so he had to tread slowly until he reached a pig pen. He watched them gobble down the food in the trough, their big, upturned noses getting dirtier as they stuck their faces in their food. Stanley watched engrossed for a while.

Out of nowhere, Stanley saw a shadow move in the farmhouse. Ignoring the pigs, he drew closer towards the house again and peered through the window, his hands placed either side of his face to block out the light and look. There was a man he did not recognise crying in the parlour. It looked like he was holding something in his hands, but they were clenched too tight to know. The man looked up, saw Stanley and ran into another part of the farmhouse. Stanley made his way to the front door and knocked loudly. There still came no reply. Not wanting to waste any more time on a house with no response, he headed back down the hill to continue his other witness interviews.

As he was walking down the hill, Mr. Richards and Llewellyn were walking up to the farmhouse. Stanley stopped them.

'I've been looking for the two of you, on police business, of course.' Stanley tried to sound authoritative but there was a definite shake in his voice. He saw the height of Llewellyn and straightened his back to try and lengthen his frame. It didn't work.

'Where were you on the night that Margaret Williams was strangled to death?' He posed the question to Mr. Richards first.

'Stanley. No need to be so formal. We cared for Margaret. I was away on farm business, lots of people will have seen me leave the village, I think I spoke to Mr. Bullins on my travels. He'll vouch for me,' Mr. Richards replied.

'I'll be the judge of that,' Stanley told him. 'And when did you return?'

'Right before the church service.' Mr. Richards nudged Llewellyn to answer the same original question.

'I was at the farm on my own all evening.' Llewellyn mumbled his reply.

'Right. Can I ask was Margaret carrying your baby?' Stanley wanted to know more.

'She might well have been, yes. But I do not know for certain.' Llewellyn's mumbled replies were fast becoming inaudible. His head gradually fell down towards his chest again as he spoke.

'Speak up, Llewellyn, please.' Stanley asked him, standing taller again to try and match Llewellyn's height. 'When did you last see your estranged, pregnant girlfriend?'

'Well, hang on a minute,' Mr. Richards stepped in. 'That's unnecessary. They were not courting.' Stanley glared at Llewellyn, raised an eyebrow and gave a slow nod.

'I see. Llewellyn, when did you last see Margaret?'

'I think I saw her last Sunday at church. We haven't spoken since she left the farm, although I heard her speaking in the inn loudly about me being a neglectful father. Baby hasn't even been born, and I don't know if it was even mine.'

'Well, it never will be now. Born.' Stanley looked straight at Llewellyn as he spoke. Llewellyn ignored him. Stanley knew he would have to be sharp and keep a mental note of everything said to ensure he would not forget anything significant.

'Who is the man crying in your house? He will not answer the door to me.' Stanley asked.

'Ah, that will be my farm worker, David. The first thing you should know about David is that he is deaf. I can assure you that he would not have deliberately ignored a police officer at the door. He's sensitive, caring, and has taken Margaret's death hard,' Mr. Richards replied.

'Oh, I see. He looked like he was holding something. A smallish item, I couldn't see through the glass.' Stanley pushed the questions further and started to sidle up to Mr. Richards, in an effort to appear more friendly now he was getting some answers out of the men. Mr. Richards promptly stepped away.

'The spoon,' Llewellyn mumbled.

'What?' Stanley asked, puzzled.

'David made Margaret a love spoon for Valentine's Day and she thought I had made it. I never corrected her,' Llewellyn rolled his eyes, and tried to walk away but Stanley stepped in his way.

'So, David loved her?' Stanley asked, wide eyed.

'Oh, yes. She could talk to him through sign language, see. She knew it from her old village. I think he mistook her kindness and interaction for love.' Mr. Richards explained, his foot now tapping.

'Hmm, this is interesting, indeed. Do you think he'd kill her out of jealousy?' Stanley pursued his questions, ignoring the men's impatience to get home.

'Oh no! Why, he can't even kill an animal on the farm, insists one of us does it.'

'Although…' Llewellyn thought out loud.

'Although what?' Stanley was desperate to hear what was coming next.

'He was always staring at her, you know. Like, really staring,' Llewellyn muttered.

'Oh. Can anyone else sign with him?' Stanley asked, appreciating the lead.

'No. As far as I know, only Margaret could sign proficiently and really engage with him. I think that's why David was so taken with Margaret. She gave him a person to properly talk with,' Mr. Richards replied.

Stanley said, 'Well, this is a turn of events. Thank you, gentlemen, you have been most helpful. Are there any other men I should know about? Was she a bit like that?'

'No. She wasn't. Men took advantage of her pleasant nature.'

As Mr. Richards spoke, he gave a deathly look towards his son. He continued. 'She had a dalliance with Henry, the stable boy at the Christmas house party, but I don't think there was anything in that. I don't think there was anyone else.'

'Henry. Stable boy. Right. Thanks both of you, I'll be in touch.' Stanley was satisfied with the line of questioning, but Mr. Richards walked up the hill slowly, and Llewellyn had gone rather pale. Stanley was left feeling a bit confused about David. He could not interview him without someone to sign for him. This caused a real problem that needed some urgent investigation.

Chapter Twenty-Five

Day Two – Afternoon

After a few house visits, Stanley was re-examining his collected witness statements. Whilst lots of people had lots to say about Margaret, her character and her relationships in the village, it was apparent that no one had seen anything suspicious on the night she was murdered. At least, they weren't admitting anything to him if they had.

He went to pursue the next key witness. Henry. Henry was outside in the stables, as expected. Stanley looked him up and down and decided that Margaret definitely did not have a type.

'Hello, I have some questions about yourself and Margaret Williams.' Stanley pointed to his police badge.

'Questions?' Henry raised his eyebrows.

'I am assuming you know that Margaret was murdered?' Stanley spoke bluntly.

'No, I hadn't heard. How sad.' Henry bowed his head.

'May I ask where you were on the evening of Saturday July the thirteenth?' Stanley asked. Still trying to find his best line of questioning, Stanley tested a more casual approach with Henry, and sat down near him, as two friends would, if chatting. Only these two didn't know each other at all.

'Oh. You may. I was in the Crown that evening

with family and friends like half the village were, I imagine.' Henry ruffled his hair.

'What time did you leave and were you alone?' Stanley probed. On his way to see Henry, he had prepared the questions he wanted to ask, so no matter what Henry's reply appeared to be, the next question would be delivered in a monotone rehearsed fashion. He had used the opposite technique for the local theatre group when he auditioned, and to this day still couldn't understand why he hadn't been given a part.

'I left fairly late, but any of the other stable boys can vouch for me.' Henry shrugged his shoulders. Stanley observed that Henry's behaviour seemed nonchalant and he wrote this down.

'And when did you last see or speak to Margaret?' Stanley questioned.

'I think it was a couple of months ago now, I can't remember exactly when. We'd quarrelled slightly, actually. I warned her off Llewellyn as I knew he was at the Glebe's house a lot and she thought I was being hurtful. I wasn't trying to be. Has she really been killed? She seemed too nice for someone to want to do that to her?'

'I'm afraid she has. Thanks for your time.' Stanley jumped up from where he was sat and left the stables with Henry's alibi and one less suspect. He saw Henry's shoulders drop and a large breath escape him as he turned and walked away.

Next on the list was Parry's house. He knew he'd at least get invited in there, that was for sure! He was looking forward to having a natter with a family friend. Parry answered the knock on the door immediately.

'Ah, dear Stanley. Your father said you were starting police duty this week. I have to say young fellow; you look awfully official in that uniform. Come on in, let's have a natter, I may have something for you.'

Stanley wiped his feet at the door as he was muddy from being at the stables.

Parry walked back into his house and Stanley followed smiling as he took off his hat. He was pleased to be out of the weather and in the warmth of the room.

'Terrible news, isn't it with poor Margaret.' Stanley put on his best adult voice, sounding sympathetic.

'Yes, it's fair to say that this has rocked the village. We're a quiet unassuming bunch, you know, Stan? But with a murderer on the loose who knows what type of reputation this village will get.' Parry didn't seem himself, but Stanley nodded politely.

'May I ask where you were on Saturday evening, please, Parry? Sorry, I am asking everyone.' Stanley sounded as official as he could when asking a family friend.

'Yes. I was in The Crown Inn until around eight and then I walked home. I do have some news for you, Stanley. On the way home I spotted Llewellyn and Margaret having what looked like a heated argument. He had been in The Crown, as well, drinking heavily. Pint after pint. He looked absolutely distraught. There were rumours that evening that Gwen was also pregnant with his baby. He spoke to no one, was alone and so angry. Each empty glass seemed to get slammed on the bar even harder. Anyway, he left the Crown right before me, but as I left, I could hear shouting. Margaret was walking along the pathway towards the church; she was holding a basket with something in it. They were arguing on the edge of the graveyard. He said to Margaret, 'Stay away from me, woman,' and she said, 'How dare you, future husband! Oh no, wait, that was all a lie.' He replied, 'Gwen is pregnant. That's my baby.' Margaret's face fell and she clutched her bump. He spat at her. 'Yours won't be mine. It's no secret you are a village whore. Needed my go, didn't I?' She was hysterical, shaking her head, crying, 'No, no, it was only you, only you.' He lunged towards her; she darted back and headed back down the way she must have come. I couldn't see much more as this was in the shadows by the church, so I carried on walking home, not wanting to be seen by either of them, like.'

Stanley had been frantically trying to retain all of this information and using his pencil, he took down some rushed notes.

'Thank you, Parry. If this progresses, would you testify in court?' Stanley was quick to warn Parry about the significance of what he saw as a witness.

'Yes. That is definitely what I saw and heard.'

Parry was adamant and shrugged.

'Thank you. I'll be in touch.'

The two men shook hands before Stanley took

leave and, heading back towards the village, purely by chance, Stanley bumped into the new milkmaid of Gellia Farm.

'Hello, Miss.' Stanley was chipper.

'What do you want?' The milkmaid, Victoria, stopped herself from walking on and slightly lost her balance. Stanley smirked at her discomfiture.

'Am I right in thinking that you are the new milkmaid at Gellia Farm?' he asked.

'Who's asking?'

Stanley stood up straighter. The girl reminded him of Mrs. Evans and her opinion of him! What an attitude this girl had. He asserted his authority.

'I am the lead police officer, responsible for finding Margaret's killer.' After Parry's statement, nothing could ruin Stanley's mood as he bounced lightly on and off his heels.

'Well yes, I used to do odd jobs here and there, but after Margaret left, they asked me to take over as full time milkmaid.' Victoria flicked her hair underneath her bonnet and maintained a deathly stare towards Stanley.

Stanley looked pleased with himself. 'And has Llewellyn ever tried to kiss you?'

'What? No, of course not!' She shook her head.

'Was he at Gellia Farm all night on Saturday?' She shook her head again.

'No, he wasn't. He was necking pints at the inn for most of it. Ask anyone in the village, except Mrs. Evans maybe.'

Stanley pretended to look surprised and opened his mouth as if to gasp but it was all an act. He was trying to keep as much as possible private.

'Thank you, Miss, that's all.' Stanley was headed home. He'd found his murderer after only five houses. What a fantastic attribute to the police voluntary service he was.

Not one to miss specific people, he headed down to the canal works. Although Stanley thought it to be unlikely that the canal men had seen anything, he wanted to be thorough in his investigations and decided to pay them a visit; after all, they all probably knew Margaret, and he was not going to leave any stone unturned.

'Good day, gentlemen!' Stanley was cheery.

'Hello, can we help you?' Jack was friendly in his reply, too.

'It's about the murder, Margaret's murder. Did you see anything on Saturday night?' Stanley looked at the gentlemen who all equally looked calm and relaxed about this line of questioning.

'Unfortunately, not, officer. We all wrapped up early that day due to the bad weather, Jack sent us home early evening.' Bryn spoke up first, and the other men nodded in collaboration.

Stanley asked, 'And you definitely didn't see anything suspicious? Or anyone out and about that you wouldn't normally see?'

'No, not that night, everyone was indoors due to the bad weather, either at home or at the inn. We made our separate ways home.' Bryn shrugged.

'Can you all be accounted for your whereabouts that evening?' Stanley was not finished yet.

Bryn started, 'Yes, I was at Coombe Lodge with

Mr. Tennant where I am staying.'

Jack added, 'I was with Alice.'

The other men mumbled their alibis. Stanley was now satisfied. 'Thank you, gentlemen, for your time.'

Later that day, Parry decided to visit the scene of the murder. He was eager to find anything that could further implicate Llewellyn, now he had given some evidence against him. The marshland was growing crispy underfoot as the mud dried and smudged itself into the grass. It crunched beneath the weight of his shoes. Parry was stamping on the ground, pacing around the area and looking desperately for a breakthrough.

A sudden crunch alerted Parry that someone was approaching. He saw a man coming down the hill. Parry did not recognise him so stepped away with his arms out wide.

'I say, do not come any closer, boy!' Parry pushed his arms out in front of him as a type of warning. He could not understand why this man was ignoring him and choosing to continue his walk to the murder scene without any consideration.

'Stay away.' He shouted at the man again who continued to ignore this request.

As the man approached, Parry watched him study the scene. Parry then chose to take no notice of him and started to scramble around in the ground frantically searching for something, well, anything. The man lingered, still saying nothing but watching his every move.

Parry marched up to him. 'I don't know who you are, boy. But I don't like you being here. You are not welcome right now.' He looked the man up and down. 'Not a policeman. Why don't you speak? Talk to me!'

The man waggled his fingers in a way that Parry had never seen before. What was this man doing and why wasn't he replying to him? The strange man pointed and waved his hands, until he looked down, and gave up. Parry had lost his patience by now.

'What is this finger waggling that you do? Speak up, boy!'.

The man faced Parry and looked at him. Parry, still wound up, got right up close to his face to try and frighten him. 'If you tell anyone I was here, boy, you will be the next one in the ground.'

The strange man walked away. About time, too.

David, unsure what Parry had tried to say to him, decided to go and visit Rosie to tell her what had happened. It was not worth dragging the Richards's into this. David knew he had been threatened; the body language and hard face of Parry had made that clear enough.

It was only a short walk, past the vicarage, Parry's house, and Coombe Lodge, before David arrived at Mackworth Hall. No knock on the door was necessary as Rosie saw him lingering outside and rushed out to meet him.

'D, I am so sorry about M,' she signed. He nodded.

'R, I have to tell you something.'

It was Rosie's turn to nod. She pointed to a bench for them to sit together in the garden. David knew that Rosie required full concentration when it came to sign language and did not want the Lodge to disturb her. Thankfully, Margaret had taught her enough, and she was learning more from David every time they bumped into each other. David relayed to Rosie everything that had happened. She managed to understand what he was telling her. She also understood why he told her and not the Richards family, who could use this to their advantage. As he finished, they both sat together, not moving.

Rosie then signed, 'We have to tell Stanley.'

David shook his head; he used his thumb and index finger and moved them a short way across his neck. 'You want to tell Reverend Isaac,' Rosie asked.

Rosie disappeared inside for a moment and returned confirming that it was cleared with her housekeeper that she was permitted a small break. They made their way back through the village and headed to the vicarage. As always, the reverend was kind, letting them both in and speaking to Rosie. David couldn't work out what was being said, but as Rosie squeezed David's hand, he concluded that it must have been something kind about their newfound friendship. David smiled.

Rosie retold David's story for him to the reverend, who raised his eyebrows at Parry's actions. David sat, hands clasped, unable to lift his head. The past couple days had been some of the saddest in his life.

Reverend Isaac was quick to reassure them both that he would go straight to the Judge with this information. He did not share that he had seen Stanley with Parry earlier and Stanley had looked particularly pleased with himself. There was definitely a suspicion that Parry had given Stanley a lead on the case. It was reassuring to see that his trusted position as vicar was making him already more approachable than the police. This encouraged him that he was doing the right thing to investigate this murder himself. Rosie and David appeared to be satisfied with Reverend Isaac's response and reassurance as they said their goodbyes and headed off back to their respective workplaces, to see the rest of the day through. Reverend Isaac wrote a note to the Judge as a word of warning about Parry Birch as a witness. Something told him that it may be the thing it needed to halt Stanley in his tracks.

Letter sent, he put his feet up to try and relax for the rest of the day. Everything had been prepared for the funeral tomorrow, apart from the grief that the village would be haunted by, particularly with a murderer still to be caught.

Chapter Twenty-Six

Day Three

Reverend Isaac woke up and immediately remembered today was the day of Margaret's funeral. He hadn't slept well the night before, constantly feeling restless, tossing and turning and wanting to get this day quickly over with. Although he was an experienced vicar, this would be the worst funeral of his life, and career. This would be the one that he'd struggle through, and hold it together, the most. He shivered. The bells would ring in approximately thirty minutes so there was no time to waste. He got dressed as though it was another day. Only it wasn't. He knew he had to be methodical and stick to his usual routine, or everything would fall apart; him, mostly. With thoughts shifting back on how to solve the case, he was also disappointed to be losing a day's worth of investigations, but his duty came first. It always did. He sighed as he straightened up his clothes and left the vicarage.

Unlike usual funerals, Reverend Isaac stood outside the front of the church and greeted the attendees. He usually hid in the back, so he didn't get caught into any awkward conversations. However, he had his detective duty as well as his clerical duty today. That was always on his mind. A notepad had been snuck into his uniform. To keep up appearances, he was polite to everyone who entered the church whilst maintaining a suspicious eye.

The ladies' black hat bands flapped in the wind, but the weather stayed dry with a chill to the air. The entire village arrived at exactly the same time, and all were wearing their mourning clothes as they swept across the churchyard path as if one swarming black cloud. Also unusually, it was agreed that twenty-seven bells would ring out, one for every year of Margaret's life, and one extra as a recognition to her unborn baby. The bellringers arrived and headed up the winding, narrow steps to the bell chamber in order to take their place for the start of the funeral. The villagers were keen to show a united front and thought this musical signal would ring out their anger and hurt in a way they were struggling to vocalise. They wanted it as a warning to the murderer that Margaret would not be forgotten.

The church was filled with candles in every spare spot possible; their flickering flames brightly lit up the church and reflected on the vast vaulted ceilings and beams. The congregation calmed as they took to their seats inside the church and waited for Reverend Isaac. He stood and waited for the bells. Twenty-seven bells slowly rang out. In the same rhythmic motion, the coffin was brought in by men of the village, and they walked down the aisle. The local male voice choir stood up and sang 'Rock of Ages'. The music spoke for their pain.

Reverend Isaac could feel his eyes filling with tears but adopted a professional veneer promptly as he knew he had to be there for his grieving parishioners. This wasn't about him. It couldn't be. He blinked hard and wiped his eyes with his sleeve. Hopefully no one would notice. Margaret's parents had travelled to the village and took the front row. They could not look up but stared at the floor throughout. Songs were mournfully sung, readings read. It didn't feel enough for such a character. It would never be enough. Reverend Isaac, however, ended on a powerful message.

'We have seen today the love and compassion this village has for dear Margaret and although she was only with us in this village for over a year of her twenty- six, she will remain in village hearts forever. I will find justice. Her and her baby will rest in peace. If you, the murderer, are in this church at this moment, you have been warned. We are a small community with a large voice and we will find justice!'

The last few words were spoken loudly and echoed around the church. The congregation unexpectedly applauded the reverend, who by this time suddenly felt hot, and his cheeks were flushed.

The reassurance the congregation gave however, settled him back down quickly as the coffin was led back out of the church towards Margaret's final resting place. The bellringers rang out another twenty-seven tolls in honour of Margaret and the baby. Reverend Isaac took a deep breath and headed outside for the burial. A few words and a prayer were spoken as they laid Margaret into her final resting place. The group of mourners all bowed their heads and gave a minute's silence to the murdered milkmaid. Her parents remained inconsolable and clung to each other tightly.

Reverend Isaac saw Stanley hovering, waiting for the funeral to end, in the corner of the churchyard. He kept peering round the corner before identifying his most opportune moment. The congregation started to slowly disperse from the graveyard. Stanley was almost springing on the spot at what he was going to do next.

Mrs. Evans was one of the few not in attendance at Margaret's funeral. It was no surprise to anyone that she had not been there as Mrs. Evans had never minced her words when it came to her disdain for Margaret. Knowing that everyone would be at the funeral, she had concocted a plan. This was an opportunity too good to miss.

Mr. Jenkins, of the Cambrian newspaper could not believe his luck. A villager in St. Catwg actually prepared to speak about Margaret. Thinking ahead, he got one of the young lads to attend the funeral, in case there was anything of note to mention there. On hearing the bells at the funeral, he knocked on Mrs. Evans door.

Mrs. Evans smiled sweetly at the young man and invited him into her parlour. Mr. Jenkins appreciated this interview and was overly warm to Mrs. Evans who was in her finest clothes, looking even smarter than her usual presentation.

Tea had been poured and Mr. Jenkins started interviewing Mrs. Evans, who was eager to talk.

'So, what can you tell us about Margaret, Mrs. Evans?'

'Well, where do I start, at the beginning one does, I suppose. Margaret came to the village last July and the whole village appeared to be enraptured with her. The men were swooning over her, and the women wanted to be her friend. I never understood the fuss myself. One of the first things she said was that she wanted to befriend the reverend - he was even teaching her to read and write you know, most improper for a woman to be learning these things. She was a milkmaid - and I will say this for her - she was brilliant with the animals. I always thought she was better with the cows than the people of this village, actually.'

Mr. Jenkins scribbled away at Mrs. Evans' admission and probed her on the murder.

'Mrs. Evans, where were you on the night that Margaret was killed?' he enquired.

'Oh, Mr. Jenkins, I was tucked up in bed, here alone, didn't hear or see a thing unfortunately. It's awfully frightening as a woman of a certain age to feel vulnerable and unsafe in your own village. I have never felt it in all my years. I hope they find him.'

Mrs. Evans tutted into her teacup and took another slurp of tea. She was enjoying her moment.

'Who do you think killed Margaret?'

There was a silence for some time, and it was clear Mrs. Evans was doing this for dramatic effect. Mr. Jenkins repeated his question.

Mrs. Evans knew she had a captive audience.

'I heard what you said, dear. I'm thinking. I know how much talk there is about Llewellyn at the moment. I'll say this. That man I have known for every single day of his life and he is clearly innocent. I know people are saying otherwise, and I know him and Margaret had something going on, but I will plead his innocence. I've never trusted another man at the farm who would have lived with Margaret. David, his name is. Deaf. But Margaret could sign for him, so he took to her. I watched him, watching her a lot actually. I feel like there may be more of a story there, if people can sign and get it out for him. Do you know sign language, Mr. Jenkins?' The interviewee had tried to become the interviewer, but Mr. Jenkins was not going along with this.

He shook his head and uttered, 'Do continue, please Mrs. Evans.'

'Well, I think I've identified one other suspect that everyone else seems to have forgotten about. Henry. A stable boy that Margaret had a dalliance with back at Christmas time. Apparently, only a few weeks later he was heard bad mouthing Llewellyn and fell out with Margaret. A jealous man is always a suspect in my mind, Mr. Jenkins.'

In response to this information, Mr. Jenkins nodded in all the right places.

'Mrs. Evans, did you think Margaret was pregnant with Llewellyn's baby?' he asked.

'Why, no, Mr. Jenkins. You see, as I have already mentioned, she was seen kissing Henry at her farm for all to see and who knows what her and David may have got up to whilst up at the farm alone. Very few would know what they were signing to each other. Margaret charmed the men; it's why she didn't like me. I saw through her charm. Do you not find it unusual, Mr. Jenkins, that a twenty-six-year-old unmarried woman would suddenly leave her home and arrive here, where she knew no one?'

Mr. Jenkins considered the question as Mrs. Evans stared and beamed at her interviewer, glad of the attention and spotlight on her. She couldn't wait to tell her friends that she'd be in the paper. The journalist was hanging on her every word, so she knew she'd performed well. Just as she planned.

A commotion outside suddenly distracted Mrs. Evans. Stanley had been loitering outside the church for some time, but now this looked like something significant was about to happen. Mrs. Evans neglected all of her manners and, forgetting that Mr. Jenkins was in her house at all, grabbed her walking stick to stand outside and watch first hand whatever was about to unfold. Mr. Jenkins soon caught on, so followed her out onto the front porch with his notepad and pencil poised for information. Both looked at each other, recognising that something serious at the funeral was about to occur. And they had front row seats to witness it all. It didn't get much better than this. She looked on, ready.

Stanley found his chance as he spotted Llewellyn walking out with his father and ran up to him. He spoke loudly, ensuring that everyone in the surrounding area would hear this declaration.

'Llewellyn Richards, I am arresting you on the suspicion of the murder of Margaret Williams. You will come with me now and you will be taken to Neath gaol until you are called for trial at Glamorgan Court of Great Sessions.' Stanley grinned, handcuffing this man who faced up to him.

The congregation gasped in unison as a type of echoed response to the arrest. Mrs. Evans stood quivering in shock from across the street, Mr. Jenkins was too engrossed in the action to even notice her. Llewellyn looked towards his father for support. Mr. Richards was quick to respond.

'You cannot do this; you have no evidence. My son was at home that evening.'

Whispers soon went around the rest of the congregation that Llewellyn was actually in the Crown that evening and plenty of other witnesses besides Parry had seen him grimacing and drinking at the inn.

'I'm afraid, Mr. Richards, that your son is a liar!' Stanley grinned.

Mr. Richards' face fell as he heard all the shouts and cries surrounding him, supporting the arrest, and looked around for support for Llewellyn, but found none.

Stanley began to haul Llewellyn away, whilst the accused man looked at his father, who was now shouting at the policeman. Reverend Isaac put his hand on Mr Richards' shoulder.

'We'll sort this.'

Mrs. Evans remained frozen on the spot. Margaret's parents lingered at the church entrance not knowing what to do. The arrest had come at a strange time and didn't make sense to most. Mrs. Evans overheard Margaret's parents discuss staying at the Crown for a few days more so they could stay around for the trial and hopefully reach a conclusion to this devastating state of affairs. Her legs were even more stiff than usual, and Mrs. Evans couldn't work out if that was all the sitting with the journalist, or the shock arrest. She watched the crowd make their way to the inn to further pay their respects to Margaret and her unborn baby. Margaret's parents walked slowly towards the inn, much further behind the rest of the group and tried to hold it together, leaving their beloved in the ground behind them. Margaret's mother let out a huge cry and her husband consoled her. Mrs. Evans couldn't imagine how it must feel to bury a child.

It had appeared that the church had emptied; only it hadn't. Gwen, Llewellyn's latest lover had run back into the church after she heard Stanley outside. She decided to stay away from the gossip. She recalled the chain of events that led to this moment. The day of the murder, she had told Llewellyn that she, too, was pregnant. Gwen had believed Margaret when she said that she was carrying Llewellyn's baby as Gwen knew how much of a charmer he could be. Her new engagement ring twirled round her finger. She had somehow got more of a commitment from him than Margaret had managed. Neither of them had told anyone yet; they had wanted to wait until Margaret had calmed down or gave up telling everyone she was having Llewellyn's baby. She didn't know he was in the Crown that same night of the murder. Doubts crept in her mind at an alarming rate. Gwen prayed harder than she ever had before.

With the churchyard now empty, Reverend Isaac knew duty meant he probably should have joined the congregation in a toast to Margaret, but he unusually wanted to be alone with his thoughts. Today had been an overwhelming day. He trundled home, hoping to go unnoticed. A noise that sounded like someone shout for him was heard, but he ignored it as if he hadn't heard them and sped up to go round the corner and get home. Reverend Isaac gave his door a hard push, it had been sticking lately. He sat back in his armchair and took notes of anything he thought was worth noting of the day.

Margaret had a lovely send off, and it was a fitting tribute to a woman he had thought so highly of. His devastation and determination for justice were unfaltering. The notepad was retrieved as he processed the day. There were two men he hadn't seen before lurking in the back and both had snuck in as the funeral started. Also, he noticed Margaret's friend, Alice, had a new gentleman friend. That man was very tall. Nothing particularly caught his attention, though, not this time although he noted down this discovery. Reverend Isaac was physically drained from the day, but his mind would not stop and was in overdrive. He paced up and down his parlour, replaying the funeral over and over, trying to think of anything that could be significant. The harder he thought, the more he reached a blank. He smacked his fist on the kitchen table. This outburst was most unusual as he gave in to his emotions but today was an exceptional circumstance and he let it happen. This needed a conclusion and he was determined to ensure justice was served. Now with the arrest, another family were now in torment. Reverend Isaac slammed his notepad on the table, reached for his candle and headed up to bed. Tomorrow was another day.

Chapter Twenty-Seven

Day Four

Reverend Isaac rattled around in his vicarage alone. As he adjusted his clerical collar, he realised that he had always wanted a sense of purpose, to be relied upon, praised even. Being a vicar was a thankless task; whilst his parishioners were mostly loyal, that didn't always feel enough. He sighed as he thought back to her greeting on her last day alive, full of life and character. He recalled the day's events. Mr. Jones had asked her to go and get a sheep's head for supper. Reverend Isaac saw her on route, and she looked as she always had. Possibly a little chubbier round the face as she was a few months pregnant, but definitely still as jolly. She did her usual wave and greeting. He worried that living with Mr. Jones would dampen her spirits, but Mr. Jones had looked after Margaret, taken her in and cared for her well under the difficult circumstances. Another sigh escaped his mouth again over the whole sorry affair. The memory of Margaret skipping her way to the twmpath barn dance was a complete contrast to the lifeless body he found only a few days ago.

Quick for a resolution, the police had arrested young Llewellyn, but Reverend Isaac knew in his gut this was wrong. He shook his head, dropped himself down into his armchair, took a long, slow gulp of his brandy and left the pages of notes he'd made on the floor by his feet. The vicarage was always untidy, but with so much on his mind, even considering picking these up was far too much effort. Dissatisfied with the actions of the police, he would have to solve this crime himself, whatever the outcome.

On a mission, he stood up, reaching for his hat and coat, and rushed out, not checking that the door had safely closed behind him. He was far too distracted in getting back outside looking for clues. Reverend Isaac knew this area so well. Every dip and groove within the land was known to him but he was slower on his feet these days, so it took him a while to get to the exact spot. As Reverend Isaac approached the area where Margaret's body had been found, he stopped, sighed and placed his hands on his hips. He couldn't believe how much rain there had been this July, but it was getting drier. Almost seeming to appear out of nowhere, a dried footprint appeared in front of him. He rushed to get his notepad out, knowing how significant this could end up being. It had to be captured. Accurately, too. He struggled to balance but placed his foot next to the footprint and saw it was noticeably larger than his own. He traced the pattern and made a note of dimensions. Time was spent to get the outline right. This could be nothing, but it could also be everything.

He was heading home when he bumped into Mrs. Evans. She hadn't been at the funeral. Reverend Isaac remembered their earlier conversation when she declared that she was no hypocrite and it was no secret that she had taken an instant dislike to Margaret. The garden gate was closed behind her and without her walking stick, Reverend Isaac noticed, she marched up to him, waving her arm in front of her, as if to flag him down.

'They've arrested our Llewellyn, Reverend! I saw it all from here. Nasty business the lot of it, isn't it? We all know it wasn't him, don't we, Reverend? That lad couldn't hurt a fly, couldn't hurt a fly, I tell you.' She used her finger to point in a direction that seemed to lead to nowhere. Reverend Isaac could tell Mrs. Evans was fast becoming distressed and needed to be calmed quickly. He cleared his throat and looked sympathetically towards her, lowering himself a little so as to maintain eye contact with the little old lady.

'Mrs. Evans, believe me, under the eyes of God, I do not trust the police, nor do they know this community as I do. I will be the one to get justice for our Margaret here, I will see that Llewellyn, nor any other innocent party will come to harm in this process.' He patted her on the shoulder and she smiled, muttered something about a pot being on to boil, then hobbled back into her house.

Llewellyn had been locked up in his small cell at Neath gaol for days, hours. He couldn't cope a second longer. There was barely an inch to move at all except to drum your fingers or tap your foot. But that wasn't enough. All of a sudden, he heard his name and with force, he was dragged out of his cell. They were taking him to court. He stood in the docks, shaking. He blinked repeatedly, trying to adjust to the new, lighter surroundings. Having never been in a court before, he looked around, desperate to focus on something. A Judge shouted which distracted him.

'Name'.

Llewellyn jumped and replied, 'Llewellyn Richards.'

The Judge eyed him most curiously and continued, 'And what is your crime, Mr. Richards?'

Llewellyn replied so quietly that the Judge must have thought that he had not responded.

'Well, you must have done something to be here, boy.'

Llewellyn stayed calm. 'I've been accused of murder, Judge. But I haven't done nothing.'

The gavel smacked against the table. 'Judges and a jury are in place to be the judge of that, boy, not you. So, you're the Miss Williams case.' Judge Woods stared at him slowly up and down again. Stanley was called to the witness box, and Llewellyn was dragged to a nearby chair.

Stanley began, 'Sir, I have witness accounts that the deceased and this man had an argument on that same night she died. He did not believe that she was pregnant with his child, your Honour. I believe we have enough evidence to prosecute.' Stanley looked smug with his statement.

'Very well, we will go to trial. I'll sort a jury for first thing tomorrow. Take him back to his cell.' Judge Woods stayed seated as Stanley and

Llewellyn exited the court. Llewellyn saw Stanley leave out the front door and wished that he had the same exit route.

He was taken back to the cell that he was desperate to never see again. The key rattled as it turned the lock and he was left alone.

Llewellyn sank into the corner and sat kneeling, head in his hands. He took a deep breath, thinking of Gwen standing alone in the church at the funeral. How he missed her and needed her soothing words that everything would be all right. Llewellyn thought of both of his unborn babies that night. One dead, one being nurtured to life. Margaret would have made a wonderful mother. It was unbelievable how someone was so in tune with nature as Margaret was. She was the best milkmaid he'd ever seen, intuitive, kind and warm. Thoughts of previous months flooded back and rolled around in his mind. It was clear that it was out of character for her to do what they had done together. He had to prove his innocence and get back to supporting his father on the farm. Under no circumstances was he prepared to hang for a crime he did not commit. There was no option but to fight and that was what he intended to do. The Richards men were not ones to give up. He smiled in the darkness.

Gwen, wanting to feel close to Llewellyn, had gone up to Gellia Farm. She wanted to sleep on his bed. No one was at the farm on her arrival, but Llewellyn had shown her where a key was kept for times like these. Well, times when Llewellyn would come home - this time was uncertain.

She lay on his bed for a while and started to imagine her life living here on the farm. They would be married, children running around. Mr. Richards would be slowly swaying in his rocking chair. Picturing the scene, she played with her dark, raven hair, twiddling it around her finger. It was frayed at the ends. Looking around, she realised how much work Margaret had put in to keep this house in top shape and how much it had deteriorated since her departure.

Gwen couldn't stay laying down, she soon became restless. Floors were swept, the kitchen cleaned and the fire stoked; everywhere dusted down. Not sure what to do next, Gwen went back into Llewellyn's room and saw his clothes had been scattered everywhere. Most were filthy, too. Gwen piled them up on the bed, with the intention of making a start on the laundry. She dared not enter Mr. Richards' room, but on creeping up to the door and having a peek in, soon recognised that father and son were alike in living conditions. Her eyes rolled and her sleeves were scrunched up as she started the laundry activity. Knowing her father back at home and seeing Llewellyn regularly slip weird and wonderful things into his pocket, Gwen knew to check his pockets first. By dusting down the sixth pair of his trousers, Gwen was fed up. By the seventh pair, she found something scrunched in the corner of his pocket. A handkerchief. MW. Gwen gasped and dropped it to the floor. He had a handkerchief of Margaret's. She had never seen him with this before, nor could it have accidently been lying around to be that deep into his pocket. Gwen felt a fool. She immediately dropped everything, ran to the front door, locked it securely, hid the key in its usual hiding place and ran.

Chapter Twenty-Eight

Day Five

The court gallery was hushed. Llewellyn was dragged into the court and pushed into his seat as the accused. He couldn't remember the last time he had managed more than a total of one hour's sleep, and with such small rations of food in there, his trousers were much looser and nearly falling down. Hunched over, he sat slumped, looking at no one and nothing. He knew who would be in the room and couldn't stand to look at them whilst he was in this state. Not until he was proven to be not guilty, which he had to be. The Judge rambled on with the proceedings; Llewellyn, not paying much attention, remained wriggling in his seat wanting to get it over with. 'Parry Birch' was being called, and Llewellyn jumped at the noise. He was not entirely convinced he had not drifted off to sleep as he was exhausted with the noise in the cells and the worry of today. Llewellyn saw that Parry looked white as he approached the court.

Parry stood in the witness box and felt everyone's staring eyes on him. He was of slender build, but the towering of the box and the height of the judge and the busy nature of the gallery made him feel like an ant where the entire colony were against him. His small frame was shrunken as his shoulders hunched and his head lobbed down towards his chest. Parry wasn't used to attending court. His dark, unblinking eyes darted in every direction possible, avoiding Llewellyn's stare.

'State your name, for the record.' Judge Woods' voice boomed.

'P – P - Parry B – B – Birch, sir,' he stammered. Parry's throat felt so dry and tight it was as if a large egg was lodged in there. He'd never stammered in his life before. He could not believe that he was struggling to get his own name out in a court.

'Thank you, Mr. Birch. I'd like you to tell the Jury exactly what you told Stanley about the night of Saturday the thirteenth of July.' Judge Woods was authoritative.

Parry took another look around the court. He'd never been in a court before. He felt uncomfortable wearing borrowed trousers from his neighbour as he'd never needed a smart pair of trousers in his life. His greying, black hair bounced on the top of his head and the carefully combed look was becoming wilder, as he ran his shaky hand through it, once then twice. Silvery wires of hair sprung out above his ears, like misplaced cat whiskers.

'I – I – I was heading home from the Crown Inn that evening. It was getting dark.' He tugged at his white shirt collar as if hoping this give him more air. It didn't seem to work. His shirt was tucked in meaning that most of the dark stains were hidden. He'd tried to angle it as such that any dirty patches were hidden. This even included not doing up the buttons entirely correctly to try and cover up how mucky it looked.

'Llewellyn had been in the inn all night, necking pint after pint.'

Parry felt the need to mime this action by lifting a hand to his mouth, then down and back up repeatedly. He suddenly felt conscious of his hands and wondered what the jury might think. The hands were crusty, hard and looked sore. It was clear he'd been a labourer in his working years, and he wondered if they may judge him for it.

'Llewellyn left, and shortly after, I also headed home. Towards the church, I heard some shouting, so stopped to see what was happening.' He seemed to have gained a little confidence as he retold his account, but the nerves would not leave him.

'I lingered on the other side of the road and listened. I saw Margaret and Llewellyn, the accused having a huge argument about the baby. Llewellyn told Margaret that his new lover Gwen was pregnant.' He paused and smirked, his mouth curving to the left-hand side of him where the Jury were seated. A few cracked teeth peered out the corner of his mouth. Parry was rather smug to declare the news that had clearly not reached village ears - until now.

From the gallery, Gwen let out a large sob, placing her hands in front of her face and ran out of the court. Parry was shaken by Gwen's reaction, not realising she was in the room and shrunk back into his shell, no longer wanting to talk.

'Continue, Mr. Birch.' Judge Woods declared, looking bored.

'Well, he said, 'and I quote Judge, *'You and your*

baby, if there is one, are dead to me, Miss Williams.' More people then left the inn so I couldn't stay behind the tree any longer, so I marched back home.'

'Did you see Mr. Richards touch Miss Williams?' The jury looked interested on this line of enquiry.

'No, sir. But they were close.' Parry answered as best he could.

'But there was no contact that you saw, Mr. Birch?' Judge Woods repeated.

'No, sir.' Parry was consistent.

'And may I ask why you visited the scene of the murder on the day after Miss Williams was found?'

Rosie gasped in court. Reverend Isaac smiled. Hearing and seeing these responses, Parry turned his head from left to right in quick succession, not knowing how to answer or what to say. Nothing at all came from out of his mouth.

'Well?' Judge Woods pushed for an answer.

'I didn't, sir, that must be misinformation.' Parry did not know what else to say.

'So, you didn't scare and frighten a deaf gentleman from the village, David, I believe is his name?' Judge Woods looked like he was suddenly starting to enjoy himself.

Stanley's jaw opened wide.

'Deaf?'

The word came as a whisper escaping Parry's mouth. He suddenly felt weak and unsteady. The room was closing in on him.

'That's all, you may step down, Mr. Birch.' Judge Woods waved him away, appearing disinterested in anything further that Parry had to say.

Parry took a slow breath. He was starting to think that what he saw maybe would not be enough and became quivery again. He wanted to get out of these clothes. They didn't represent him. He wasn't himself.

Llewellyn was wringing his hands after Parry's testimony but could not let his feelings show as he feared it would work against him. Every single thing that man had said was a lie. Except one. It was unclear how he knew about Gwen. Llewellyn saw Gwen rush out the gallery unable to breathe, and it took every shred of willpower not to follow her out and console her. His hands scrunched up into fists. He needed to punch something but had to sit there and listen.

There were lots of hushed discussions around the court after Parry's declarations. Gwen's reaction proved Parry's words to be true and therefore it was likely that the Jury would think that Llewellyn was the last person to see Margaret alive - and the first to see her dead. Llewellyn looked across and saw that Stanley was sat on his own in the gallery, and his face was crinkled as Parry spoke through his story. But the statement appeared to be enough to raise questions to Llewellyn's actions, he could tell by the jury's reactions. Stanley's face relaxed as he sat there in his own little world.

Five more witnesses were called which proved Llewellyn was in the Crown Inn on the night of the murder. No one else had seen Llewellyn with

Margaret apart from Parry but it confirmed that Llewellyn was definitely in the inn, and not at Gellia Farm alone, as his own original statement had declared. It proved he was a liar.

Llewellyn was called next to the witness box. All of the witnesses had worn him down and feeling that he had already been proved to be a liar, he thought the jury would not trust his statement. Judge Woods started his questioning.

'Confirm your name for the record.'

He replied, mumbling, 'Llewellyn Richards, sir.'

'Speak UP, boy, or we'll never get through this.' Judge Woods was getting less patient as the trial progressed. Llewellyn looked up at the gallery and saw his father leaning forward in the front row, hands clasped in a prayer position between his legs. Gwen had not returned. Llewellyn turned back towards the Judge and looked at him, waiting.

'Where were you on the night of Saturday the thirteenth of July?' Judge Woods asked.

'I was at the farm for most of the day, and then early evening I headed to the Crown Inn. Alone. Gwen had told me that afternoon that she was pregnant, which surprised me. I was not sure how to handle a second woman in a few months giving me such news. I didn't say much to her, so she left. I wanted to drink. I needed a drink.' Llewellyn stuck to the facts and answered coherently.

'Then what happened?' Judge Woods probed; the questions were being fired quicker.

'Then nothing. I got drunk, too drunk, if truth be told, sir. I wasn't drinking with anyone so I drank as much as I could afford to, probably more, and left.' Llewellyn thought back to that moment and sighed.

'And what did you say when you saw Margaret?' Judge Woods wanted a confession.

'I never saw her, sir.' Llewellyn was resolute and shook his head to reaffirm his words. There would be no confession crawling into the court's ears on this occasion. There was nothing to confess.

'So, you are calling Mr. Birch a liar?' Judge Woods questioned. The last few words sounded elevated as an echo bounced off the walls, despite the court being at full capacity.

'I am saying that he cannot have seen what he thinks he saw.' Llewellyn again sounded certain. Unlike Parry, the defendant was calm, crystal clear and knew he was telling the truth.

'Yet you say you drank too much that evening?' Judge Woods said.

'Yes. But I remember the long steep walk home, alone.' Llewellyn tried to maintain his dignity, despite what people may be thinking about him. As he stood giving his account, he wondered if he would ever make that walk home again, or if his life would be ending with these words spoken in this room today. His hands shook but he had to fight for justice.

'Did anyone stop and speak to you on your way home?' Judge Woods appeared to be getting harsher, and looked a little flustered himself, his pink cheeks becoming ruddy against the white wig.

'No.'

'Yet you are certain you did not see, or touch Margaret Williams?'

'I am.'

Stanley stared at Llewellyn in disbelief at his calm composure answering these questions. Murmurs in the gallery caused a mixed reaction. Whispers of 'Guilty' and 'Not guilty' were rising in the gallery. Judge Woods banged his gavel hard.

'Enough!'

There was a stunned silence as the court hushed in an instant. Llewellyn was back slumped in the dock. He was not sure he had done enough. Needing reassurance, he looked up at his father who wore a forced, fake smile. Llewellyn hung his head and kept staring at the floor as Judge Woods summarised the witness statements. Even the smell of the room was starting to bother Llewellyn. The place smelt dusty and old. Dead. The jury listened, fully engaged to the Judge's words. They were then told that they would be escorted to a smaller room in the court and that they were not allowed to leave until there was a unanimous verdict. As they walked out, Llewellyn realised that these twelve unknown men would be the ones to seal his fate. He was pulled from behind, made to stand. Although his stomach was twisted in knots, he was incredibly hungry as he had not eaten that morning, or the one previously. Stanley, getting far too carried away with proceedings shouted, 'Murderer' as Llewellyn stood. Judge Woods gave him a look and then Stanley remembered himself and sat back down like a chastised child keeping quiet. He sat on his hands to avoid any further outbursts. They twitched under him. This was the last thing Llewellyn saw before he was back inside a small holding cell below the courthouse.

Those in the gallery left and dispersed, having no idea how long a verdict would take. Gwen was outside, still trembling, and Mr. Richards went to speak to her.

'He loves you, Gwen. He's proving his innocence for you and your baby.' Mr. Richards tried to reassure her.

'But why does he care about my baby and didn't care for Margaret's?'

Mr. Richards replied, 'I can't say for certain, Gwen, I am not him, but his love for you seems deeper rooted than that he had for Margaret. Come back to the farm with me tonight, if you'd like, Gwen. Treat Gellia as your home.'

Gwen replied, 'No, thanks, that's what Margaret did and it didn't work out too clever for her and her baby. See you soon, Mr. Richards.' Gwen set off home. It had been an emotional day, and she now felt as vulnerable as Margaret had. She thought back to the conversation when she had told Llewellyn he was going to be a father. Gwen had heard the rumours about Margaret and believed that Llewellyn was the father of the baby... When Llewellyn's face had dropped at her news, she knew exactly how Margaret felt. Now Margaret was dead. Gwen feared for her life, not because of Llewellyn, however, she felt someone else in the village must be behind this. Parry's version of events was false, and he'd always looked at her rather strangely and made her uncomfortable. She needed to get home quickly, and ensure she couldn't stop and see that man, Parry Birch.

The jury, having been ushered into a side room, were all having conversations with one another at once. Judge Woods stepped in to give them a bit of advice.

'Unanimous, please, if possible, here. This is an important case, with a life at stake, so if you convict him, you have to be more certain than not that he did it.'

'Thanks, your Honour,' said one man. The table of men bobbed and nodded their heads in agreement with the Judge's words. He gave one last instruction before leaving them to discuss.

'Sooner the better, gentlemen, please. All night if you have to.' He shut the door behind him, leaving the men to discuss Llewellyn's fate.

'Well, that Parry chap saw something, didn't he?' One started the conversation.

'Didn't see a murder, though, did he?' Questioned another. It was to be a long night of deliberations. Judge Woods took off his wig and sat in his chamber, taking a swig of brandy. This was a difficult trial, no matter what the outcome.

Reverend Isaac was keen to go as unnoticed as possible and did not wear his clerical collar to sit in the gallery. Trying to be clever, he thought that this would test if people looked at the face or the uniform. He, of course, being a clever man with a sound mind, completely expected his disguise to fail, but actually the people in the village were so obsessed with proceedings he was allowed to disappear completely into the background. This suited him as he could look at the hard facts and ignore any hear say. Fully focussed on the case, he took out his notepad as the witnesses spoke and jotted down anything that may be significant. Reverend Isaac paused and scratched his head. He was more fidgety without his collar on, although now he was back at the vicarage it did not matter. He was not used to not being recognised as the village vicar, and certainly not used to being a detective. Needing some Holy courage, he patted his neck for reassurance that he was doing the right thing, whilst looking over at the cross that hung on the wall. A swig of brandy soon went down. Then another.

Chapter Twenty-Nine

Day Six

The next morning, Judge Woods knocked on the door and entered the jury's room.

'Have you reached a verdict?'

'We have, your Honour.'

'Is it unanimous?'

'It is.' All the men nodded their heads in agreement, in unison.

'Very well. We'll hear it at midday. Go home and make yourselves a bit more presentable. Thank you, gentlemen.' The men ushered themselves out of the room, one by one, satisfied with their verdict. Judge Woods asked someone to go to St. Catwg to ask anyone interested to be at the courtroom at midday, sharp.

Crowds seeped around the court before midday. Mr. Richards pushed and shoved himself to the front of the chaos, elbowing anyone in his way.

'This is my boy on trial.'

Margaret's parents were also in attendance, both wearing black and waited on the edge of the crowd - they were seemingly not used to such crowds and too scared to react. Judge Woods saw them and created a route to ensure they had gallery seats for the verdict. The judge was trying not to show any nerves. There had never been a hanging case in Neath before. The crowd outside and the press interest suggested there may be a hanging verdict.

Whilst heading back to his chamber, he heard a commotion in the gallery. He stopped. This wasn't the time for court drama but on stepping into the courtroom, he saw that Margaret's mother had fainted. It was a hot day, and the last few days were likely to cause physical angst. He knew she had to be well enough to hear the verdict. Quick to act, he went outside and shouted, 'Verdict delayed an hour.' The jury and gallery were notified also. Margaret's father was fanning his wife, and she slowly lifted up her head. Llewellyn had been summoned to be brought out which was then abruptly stalled. What was going on? No one had bothered to tell him anything, despite him repeatedly asking, and his life was on the line. The wait was excruciating.

Mr. Richards sat tapping his foot and this became more aggressive as the minutes continued. The crowd outside stared, waiting for the clock to chime once to know when this unforeseen delay would be over.

They waited. The crowd were silent.

The clock struck one and the crowd chanted and shouted and fell over each other, trying to hear what was going on inside now. All of the gallery seats were full. Judge Woods was in no rush for fear of what the outcome might be. He stood up and adjusted his wig and coat before approaching the court. Everyone in the room immediately stood at the sight of him but he waved his hands back down to sit. He checked on Margaret's mother before agreeing to continue. She confirmed that she was well enough for a verdict to be heard. The jury were seated. Llewellyn was brought in. He kept his head down. The court was hushed.

'You have reached a unanimous verdict, Jury?'

'We have, your Honour.'

'Is the defendant guilty or not guilty of the murder of Miss Margaret Williams on Saturday July the thirteen, eighteen twenty-two?'

The crowd was silent. The court was silent. Llewellyn felt his heart thumping quickly in his chest. It was so quiet, he was sure everyone could hear it.

'Not guilty.'

There was a unified gasp from the court. Llewellyn fell to his knees and the court descended into chaos. Heckles of 'Murderer,' could be heard over the loud sobs of Margaret's mother. Her husband was consoling her, but his jaw was tense and his fist was a tight ball. He looked flushed. Mr. Richards punched the air and leaped towards his only son. He grabbed him and held him tight.

'It's all right, son, you're coming home. You are coming home.'

Judge Woods, relieved with the outcome, believing it to be the correct one, tried to gain some structure back into the court, but failed miserably.

'Order, order!'

He banged his gavel with all his strength, but the mixed reactions of the gallery and the crowd meant no one heard him.

'Mr. Llewellyn Richards, you are an innocent man and therefore, free to leave the court.'

The Richards family were relieved to exit the court. Gwen had been waiting outside in an alley. From the corner of her eye, she saw Parry as part of the crowd and couldn't bear to be near him. On sight of Llewellyn, she leapt out of the alley and ran to him, threw her arms around him and kissed his face. Parry made an angry noise that sounded like he was in pain and sloped off, kicking the ground under him. His evidence was not enough to be rid of this man. Gwen saw Parry disappear round the corner and hugged Llewellyn even tighter.

'I love you,' she told him.

'I love you, too,' he replied.

Reverend Isaac, based on the success of yesterday, again remained in disguise of sorts. No one had noticed him, anyway. He had stayed sat in the corner of the court to avoid the crowd and to consider what had happened. It was the right decision. Based on what the court had heard, there was not enough evidence to condemn a man to death. However, he was starting to think that Llewellyn had killed Margaret. He would not tell this to anyone else, and he would not close himself off to anything else that appeared amiss, but his suspicion was shifting towards one man only.

Reverend Isaac got up to leave the court and saw that there was still a small gathering outside. He saw Gwen and Mr. Richards celebrating. Alice and her new boyfriend were there, too. They hadn't been formally introduced yet. Margaret's parents were nowhere to be seen. Margaret's father was convinced that Llewellyn had done this and as the verdict was heard, he had jumped out and shouted that he would appeal. Reverend Isaac snuck out of the back door and into Neath town centre. On the other side of the road, he caught a sheep's head looking at him and thought back to Margaret's basket. He went into the shop.

'Hello, can I help you?' The man behind the counter looked cheery and welcoming.

'Yes, you might be able to.' Reverend Isaac's mind was working overtime on how to best approach his questions without it being too obvious what he was up to.

'I hear that man got off for murder, that must be a relief, mustn't it?' The small talk after such a big case would likely go on for weeks. However, it gave Reverend Isaac a natural way in to ask questions.

'Yes, indeed it must. Did you ever serve that murdered girl one of your sheep's heads?'

'Yes, it was me personally, actually, on the night she died. She had such a warm smile and was talking about her baby. I guess now I must have been one of last few people to see her alive.'

'Oh, right. And she seemed her usual self?' Reverend hoped something would come of this, answers were needed.

'She did. Jolly, chatting, like we've always known her. Such a sorry affair. I was devastated when I realised it was her.' A frown creased across the butcher's face and his cheery manner halted in remembrance of Margaret. Reverend Isaac was starting to think that this case may never get solved as no answers were forthcoming from anyone – more so in the court room.

'Thanks, you've been most helpful. I'll buy some of these, if that's all right.' Feeling obliged now to buy something, Reverend Isaac pointed to some meat on the bottom shelf.

'Yes, of course.'

Coins were exchanged and Reverend Isaac collected his meat and went on his way. As he was headed home, he felt a hand on his shoulder.

'Lovely funeral service you gave, Reverend, how about you stick to your day job.' The words were spat in his ear.

Reverend Isaac jumped, but as he turned around no one was directly behind him. He looked all ways, but the court crowd had dispersed, and nobody was near to him. The entire walk home, Reverend Isaac felt jumpy. How had he been pounced on like that, for no one to be there? Walking home, he was vigilant but was left undisturbed by any other incident.

Stanley was looking jittery, waiting for the Reverend on his doorstep.

'Stanley. Do come in. What can I do for you?' Reverend Isaac yawned, his years after a busy day finally catching up with him, but he hoped Stanley might be useful for a change.

'I saw you taking notes at the court, Reverend.' Stanley said.

'Ah.' Reverend Isaac smiled. His disguise had not proved to be as successful as he had hoped.

'I do think Llewellyn did it, you know, Reverend.'

Stanley was resolute.

'Hmm, and why?' the vicar asked.

'Well, he was at the Crown, and it was proven in court he previously lied to me about that. We know from Parry's statement that Gwen is pregnant, and Llewellyn is the father. Her exit out of the court proved Parry found that out when no one else knew. Plus, Margaret was pregnant and had claimed it was Llewellyn's baby. He had motive. It's all impeccable timing, Reverend.' Stanley stood tall. He saw a drawing on the cluttered table. 'What's this, Reverend?' Reverend Isaac shot a look to Stanley and raced over to the table to turn it around.

'Nothing of your concern, dear boy."

'I'll ask again, what is this drawing and are you withholding evidence?' Stanley was leaning right in Reverend Isaac's face.

'I went back to the crime scene a couple of days ago and saw this in the mud. I took a sketch, in case, but then forgot about it and dismissed it, as it could have been anyone's.' Reverend Isaac was clearly not bothered by Stanley's attempt to cross examine and shrugged.

Stanley was distracted, holding up the sketch. He turned it around in different angles and kept it close, but not too close to the candlelight.

'It's his. It's Llewellyn's.' Stanley again was resolute as he stared further into the drawing.

'You have absolutely no proof of that, Stanley. You must be careful when you make accusations.' Reverend Isaac rolled his eyes.

'He's big. This is a giant shoe.' Stanley now gazed open mouthed at the discovery.

'There are lots of tall men in the village who use that same walkway, Stanley. You are fairly lanky, why, how do I know that this isn't your shoe?' Reverend Isaac decided to tease the young boy, who, by now, was getting on his nerves. Stanley immediately lifted up his shoe and looked at the detailing and size; his head turned back and forth from the sketch to the shoe. Every couple of seconds he huffed and puffed and made grunting noises. A little titter escaped Reverend Isaac's mouth.

'How dare you accuse a self-respecting police officer of such a crime. I understand the Richards family are your friends, Reverend, but you cannot have friends in this line of work. You can as a vicar, perhaps, but not as a detective.' He tried to turn his professional expertise of a few days into being a subject matter expert. Reverend Isaac was having none of this.

'Need I remind you, dear boy, that in all my years of work, I have met plenty of colourful characters and as a vicar, it is not my job to be their friend. I am here to help the community as my duty to God. You have walked into this role for two weeks only and used your case to arrest Llewellyn purely on an unreliable witness statement of a family friend of yours. You strongly need to listen to your own advice.'

Reverend Isaac paused for breath and Stanley was left stood completely dumbfounded. There was a long awkward silence in the parlour, which neither wanted to break.

'Well, I trusted you, and I wanted your help, but clearly we see this case differently, Reverend.' Stanley eventually broke the silence.

'We need some factual evidence here, Stanley, or this case will never get resolved.' Reverend Isaac responded.

'Not we. I, Reverend, I.' Stanley pointed to himself, he was shaking. 'I am the lead police officer of this investigation, and it is I who needs to see Llewellyn brought down for this. Not you.'

Reverend Isaac answered, 'I am not saying Llewellyn didn't murder Margaret, but even if he did, no one can prove it. But do consider other suspects, even if it's to rule them out. Margaret became a friendly and welcome face to the village in her short time here, and I want to see justice, no matter who did it. But without more evidence we won't get anywhere.'

Reverend Isaac sat down at his table, propping his head up with his hand. He probed Stanley further.

'Have you been to every single property in St. Catwg?' Reverend Isaac wanted to bring this case back to basics, as he was not confident Stanley had undertaken the correct action.

'I went, but not everyone was in. I have ruled out Henry, he had an alibi.'

'Well, try every single door.' Reverend Isaac volunteered.

Stanley nodded.

'Then what, Reverend?'

‘I fear, I don’t know, boy. Have you spoken to Gwen?’

Stanley looked up. ‘Her mother wouldn’t let me near her, said I caused too much upset by the court declaration.’

‘Right. Yes. Well, that was incredibly unfortunate. Do not, Stanley, I repeat, do not approach her if Gwen is alone. The women in this village are scared enough going out on their own and she is early stages of pregnancy so cannot have any further distress. Do you understand?’

‘Yes, Reverend.’

‘I will go and see her and her mother in the morning. Maybe they’ll speak to me. Being a vicar can have its advantages.’ He drummed his fingers on the table whilst deep in thought. He was so distracted he had almost forgotten that Stanley was still leaning in the doorway and as such, jumped when Stanley spoke.

‘Right, sounds like a plan here, Reverend. Thanks for listening. Let’s catch ourselves a killer.’

Reverend Isaac looked like something obvious had leaped out at him. The table felt a hard smack as he stood up.

‘Stanley?’ Reverend Isaac sounded urgent.

‘Yes?’ Stanley was less so.

‘You are not going to like this, I fear.’ Reverend Isaac said and paused.

‘Go on.’ Stanley was bouncing on the spot.

‘I think you need to speak to Parry for a second time. You may believe his statement, but the jury definitely did not. I am not entirely sure that he did see Llewellyn and Margaret arguing, as she didn't make it to the top of the hill. Which could suggest Parry was walking from the pub, home alone, without an alibi.'

Stanley's face dropped as the realisation that these words made sense. Parry was another person to revisit. Reverend Isaac rolled his eyes at the young boy's excitability when it was such a serious matter, even if the Parry admission did upset him. His bed was calling him now, so he had no energy left to dispute his behaviour.

Stanley walked back over to the table. 'I think I'll take this, if that's all right, Reverend?' He held up the sketch of the footprint.

'Yes, yes, if you must, boy.' He waved Stanley on, keen to get rid of him promptly. This didn't work, so he stood up and edged Stanley towards his door to leave. Stanley was not seeming to take the hint and was still jabbering on, much to the annoyance of Reverend Isaac.

'Well, Reverend, I'll go to see Parry again, plus I'll call at the houses I haven't been to yet, you visit Gwen. I'll hand this sketch in at the station, and we'll reconvene once we're done.'

Reverend Isaac forced a smile and edged Stanley to take his final few steps out of the vicarage. Before Stanley could say another word, Reverend Isaac slammed the door shut. Bedtime.

Chapter Thirty

Day Seven - Morning

Reverend Isaac went to see Gwen first thing that morning. He knew that the family were always up early doing their chores, so was eager to see them. When he rapped on the door, a gaunt and pale Mrs. Glebe answered, rolling her eyes. She let the vicar in and told him to sit down at the kitchen table.

'I say, are you all right, Mrs. Glebe?' Reverend Isaac looked concerned. He knew his parishioners well and something did not seem right.

'Yes, poor Gwen has been up all night, shrieking and wailing over what's happened. I haven't had a wink of sleep.' Mrs. Glebe yawned and sunk back into the kitchen chair. Gwen was also at the kitchen table, hunched over and head down on the hard surface.

'If it is too much to converse today, I can come back another day.' Reverend Isaac read the room and felt it wasn't appropriate to ask any further questions. No one responded to Reverend Isaac who by now had pushed his chair under the table and was making his way to the front door he'd only seconds ago walked through to enter. Then, from the corner of his eye, he saw Gwen throw something small across the table. It caught Reverend Isaac's eye enough to turn around fully to inspect. Gwen proceeded to sob.

'He did it,' she said between sobs.

'Who did what, Gwen?' Reverend Isaac asked softly.

'Llewellyn killed Margaret,' she confirmed.

'What is this?' he queried, spotting a familiar small piece of square cloth on the table in front of her.

'Her handkerchief. I went to the farm a couple days ago to do Llewellyn's washing. I knew no one else would bother. The new milkmaid Victoria is a right lazy miss, so I went to do it myself. I checked his pockets; I always do as there's always something in them. There it was. MW is stitched in so it must be hers. He must have taken it off her body as a souvenir. I think I am next, Reverend.' Gwen forced the words out, gulping air and puffing out her cheeks. She, like Margaret, had kept holding her tummy. Reverend Isaac bowed his head to process the information and remained calm.

'And you are sure this is new to Llewellyn's possession?' He wanted to get facts right.

'Well, I've never seen it before, and why would it appear in his trouser pockets now?' Gwen was certain. Reverend Isaac had to admit that it did seem too much of a coincidence for it not to be true with Gwen's timings. However, he did not want to panic her.

'Do you mind if I take this as evidence, Gwen? Hopefully it won't be necessary, but I want to keep you and your baby safe. I must say I am surprised at this though, the two of you seemed cosy after the not guilty verdict.'

She hesitated, then nodded. 'I was relieved the father of my baby wasn't going to be hung. But I can't get this handkerchief out of my mind.'

Reverend Isaac said, 'And for the record. He loves you, only you. He never loved Margaret, I don't think. That's the difference in the two of you. If you two can get over this rough time, you'll be very happy together.' He tucked the handkerchief into his pocket and forced a smile at Gwen. She had by now calmed slightly, and it was only when Mrs. Glebe involuntarily coughed that either Reverend Isaac or Gwen remembered that she had actually been sat listening the whole time.

She stood up. 'Thanks for coming, Reverend, you have calmed my girl down.' She moved to stand behind Gwen and stroked her hair.

'You are welcome, both. If you need me at any time, you know where I am, as always. I'll show myself out.' He headed through the parlour and out of the front door. As he shut the door, he hovered at the doorstep, for a moment. Wanting to inspect the evidence, he reached in his pocket and looked at the handkerchief. Reverend Isaac traced over the lettering with his index finger slowly. There was a smudge of mud on the edge of the corner. He scrunched it back up and put it safely back in his pocket. It was clear that Stanley would love this. Reverend Isaac headed home whilst wondering how Stanley was getting on today.

Stanley had followed Reverend Isaac's advice and returned back to the door-to-door activity where he had previously had no reply. The conversation with Parry worried Stanley so much, he put it off for as long as possible. Most people asked him why Stanley was still going door to door when it was clear Llewellyn had been acquitted - news had travelled fast in this village.

Giving his practised reply, Stanley said, 'When a defendant is found not guilty, it may be that evidence at the time of the original trial was not available, without which, it was not possible to reach a true verdict. Which is why it's so important that if you did happen to see anything at all that evening, you tell me, so we, as a village can get this murderer convicted, once and for all.' He cleared his throat.

Responses came firing back at him.

'Sorry, I was still in the Crown when he left, we all remember discussing how pleased we were that he'd gone. Didn't see anything on the way home.'

'Sorry Stanley, nothing unusual springs to mind.'

'Sorry, no, can't think of anything that happened that night.' Door shut.

One by one, door by door, Stanley drew a blank. He hoped that Reverend Isaac had got a bit luckier at Gwen's house.

After delaying the inevitable, Stanley visited Parry, who welcomed him and shook his hand.

'You lied in court, didn't you, Parry?' Stanley delivered this question as calmly as any young man could manage. It wasn't overly successful in its delivery.

'No.' Parry was a little shaky but stuck to his story. Neither spoke for what felt like minutes.

'And you are honestly sure that you saw what you

declared in court?' Stanley wanted more answers from Parry, who looked to be a defeated man.

'I am, yes.' Silence lingered in the air.

'Did you murder Margaret Williams?' Stanley had never been so serious.

'No, I didn't. I thought you were a mate, Stanley, I can't believe you're doubting me.'

'But you have no alibi?' Stanley was learning as a police officer that you cannot trust everyone immediately, and the truth must be sought.

'No. I don't.'

'I'm not sure I can trust you anymore.' Stanley stood up to leave. There was nothing else to say.

Stanley knocked at the vicarage door. He hoped that this would be the last door he knocked upon that day. Reverend Isaac ushered Stanley in.

'Come on in.'

The open-door policy had never been so prevalent in all his many years as a vicar as it had over the past seven days. Stanley made his way into Reverend Isaac's parlour and was keen to get into discussion quickly about the case.

'Unfortunately, no one at all saw anything that night. I have now completed my enquiries and asked every single person in the village if anyone saw anything. There is nothing new. And I pushed, Reverend, I pushed.'

'I understand, Stanley. Well, Gwen might have given me something. You may want to sit down for this, Stanley. Between this and Parry's witness statement, we may have something.'

Stanley proceeded to sit down as quickly as possible, keen to hear what the Reverend had to say.

Reverend Isaac did not pause to wait. 'Gwen gave me this.' He passed the handkerchief to Stanley who picked it up and stared at it for a while, without saying anything at all.

'Was this found at Gellia Farm?' he asked eventually. 'Is that where she found it?' Reverend Isaac nodded.

'It has mud on it.' Stanley clasped his hand to his mouth, taking all the information in. Reverend Isaac nodded again.

'Between this and the footprint, I think we have something. Is Gwen willing to testify against him though?' Stanley asked.

'It appears so, yes.' Reverend Isaac replied.

Stanley looked like he was about to spring up into the air, but then he remained straight faced, deep in thought. Reverend Isaac observed that the young lad held his emotions in for a change. It seemed this murder had changed everyone.

'There is something you need to know. Parry still says what he said in court is true. He also doesn't have an alibi but swears that he didn't kill her. Something about him looked altered today. He was different.' Stanley warned.

Reverend Isaac did not move and processed everything the last day had brought up. Maybe Stanley was becoming a good police officer after all, as it was not expected that he would speak against Parry or even doubt him. He wondered what was said today to make Stanley seem less sure about Parry. This case had pushed everyone to their limits. Reverend Isaac felt older than he had ever felt at that moment.

'I'm going to go to Judge Woods right away.' Stanley leapt up and, grabbing the handkerchief, rushed out the door, not even saying farewell to the reverend who, although knowing he had done the right thing, definitely felt that he hadn't. Gwen testifying against Llewellyn would not be a pleasant experience.

Stanley had raced to Neath to speak to Judge Woods. He soon realised that he was not as fit as he'd hoped and on arrival to Neath stopped, grabbed his chest and took some deep breaths and knew he would be bright red with exertion. He was glad of a slight breeze as this gave him more air. He checked his pocket for the drawing and the handkerchief before knocking on the door of Judge Woods' chamber.

'Enter,' came the booming voice from the other side of the door. Stanley hobbled in, his legs feeling stiff after his run to Neath.

'Your Honour.' Stanley bowed.

'What can I do for you on a Saturday?' Judge Woods lifted his eyes off his paperwork.

'Your Honour, I've got new evidence. Here is a drawing of a footprint at the crime scene that's been found. It shows the killer to have big feet and wearing sturdy boots, like farm boots that Llewellyn would wear. Also, Gwen Glebe has handed over a muddy handkerchief bearing Margaret's initials.' Judge Woods inspected the evidence.

'Where did you find the footprint?' he asked.

'Reverend Isaac found it and drew it, your Honour,' Stanley admitted.

'What did Gwen say when she handed this to you?' Judge Woods held up the handkerchief in question.

'Oh, well, you'd have to speak to the reverend for that, Judge, as he retrieved this from her this morning.' Stanley again was honest with the evidence; he waited for Judge Woods to declare that he could arrest Llewellyn again with a new trial.

'Right. So, it looks like Reverend Isaac is on the case, and not you, Stanley.' Judge Woods concluded.

'I have been finishing my door-to-door enquiries, your Honour.' Stanley remained positive.

'Hmm.' Judge Woods tutted. 'I've heard enough. I'm sorry, Stanley, but Llewellyn has been found not guilty already. This evidence you have provided is circumstantial at best, and I'm afraid that this is not enough to reconvict and retry an innocent man.'

Stanley replied urgently, 'But sir!' He repeatedly pointed at the footprint sketch and the handkerchief, but Judge Woods' mind was made up.

'No. No more, Stanley. Enough. Please leave and only come back to me if someone says they saw someone with their hands on Margaret.' Judge

Woods escorted him out and shut the door behind him.

Stanley sighed with his shoulders drooping and left the building. He told everyone he bumped into on the way home about this news. By the time he reached the vicarage again, Reverend Isaac had already heard. Stanley was not prepared to let this rest. It was vital that the whole village knew, and fast, exactly whom the murderer was.

Chapter Thirty-One

Day Seven - Afternoon

Llewellyn couldn't believe what had happened to Margaret, but he was innocent. Whilst he had behaved appallingly, he was not a murderer. It was that simple. Her parents did not believe his innocence, nor did half the village. Plenty of close friends and allies had been quick to judge and turn their backs on him and everyone at some point had considered him a murderer, even for a second.

He had visited her grave that very day. The church had emptied after the morning's prayers, and Llewelyn felt compelled to see Margaret. With so much attention on him in the past few days, he had not had much alone time, or time to go to the grave. It felt the right day.

Conscious he'd be seen doing this, he had now learnt not to care about what the villagers may or not be thinking after these events. He did not tell anyone where he was going, particularly his father, as he thought he'd soon try and talk him out of it. But Llewellyn's mind was made up. Arms swinging in a gesture of confidence, he trundled down the hill with an air of freedom in his step, pleased to be out and attempt to try and clear his conscience. He'd never get over this, but he felt that if he could at least apologise to Margaret, it'd go some way into making him feel better.

As he approached the grave, he had realised that

he had spotted no one on the walk down. Maybe Mrs. Evans was having a sleep, the excitement and exertion of morning prayers had probably made her tired. Llewellyn bowed his head and sat down next to the grave to be close to Margaret. It was incomprehensible that it had come to this; her radiance, beauty and light now departed into nothingness in the ground.

'Margaret.' His voice broke. He could hardly get her name out. This was harder than he had anticipated. He coughed, paused and repeated her name. 'Margaret.' It was clearer this time and he carried on. 'I hope you know that I didn't do this to you. I never would. You always called me your gentle giant. I hope you still think that even though I was so cruel to you when you told me that you were having our baby. Our baby is there with you. I hope you are looking after him. I've always thought of it as a boy. Llewellyn Junior. Although I'm sure he'd be less of a coward than me, and more ferocious like you. Who would want to harm you, Margaret? I dare not believe that anyone in this village would do this to you. I loved you, but when you told me you were pregnant, I panicked because by then I had found out I loved Gwen more. I would never wish you harm, but I never wanted you to be my wife, though, because when I fell for Gwen, I realised I loved you like a sister, not a lover and for that I'm sorry.' Llewellyn broke down, wiping away tears with the back of his large, farmer's hands. 'I keep thinking how big your bump would be right now. Or if we'd have our baby. I would introduce him to everyone and everything at the farm, and you could take him to see the cows. Our new milkmaid is horrible compared to you. We don't have the same chats, not like our chats. I am keeping my head down like before and trying to stay out of trouble. Not that I was in trouble. You hooked me in, Margaret. I fell in love with your ways instantly. Your voice was confident, but you were so scared and frightened. You looked so dishevelled with your few belongings and wispy hair, slightly out of place. Your big smile captured my heart immediately and I wanted you, or so I thought, like. I never had marriage in mind, and when you said you were pregnant, I was cruel to you. I could have let you down more gently. I think you'd be laughing at me right now, I don't think you've ever heard me say so many words in such a short space of time. You would be teasing me saying stop talking and doing your girly giggle. Oh. I miss that giggle. Margaret. I'm sorry. I want to find your killer, but I'm scared to get too involved after everything that's happened. You know I don't believe in spiritual things; I guess your Mystic Mildred reading was right, though. But, please, signpost me towards your killer. I will do my best to see you get justice.'

Two people, who Llewellyn didn't recognise, walked through the graveyard. They ignored him and walked to the grave they were visiting. Llewellyn jumped up, brushed his hands down his trousers to clear the dirt, and stopped to look at the grave one last time. He turned away, giving Margaret one last look. He knew in his heart that would be his final conversation with her. He would not visit her again. Too many eyes. It was not the same without her cheeky replies, anyway. Llewellyn could never keep up with a one-sided conversation. Unsurprisingly, as he was about to walk home, Mrs. Evans was pottering about in the garden.

'Hello,' she said brightly. Llewellyn knew then that she must have had a sleep as she was not normally that chirpy in the afternoon.

'Good afternoon, Mrs. Evans,' Llewellyn replied.

'Have you been out for a walk, nice day for it?' she asked. Llewellyn had spotted that she was eyeing him rather suspiciously, but he certainly wasn't going to confess to the village gossip on such a personal and delicate matter.

'Yes Mrs. Evans, I did a quick round the village walk, headed home now as my stomach is rumbling.'

Llewellyn patted his stomach and smiled. Mrs. Evans looked like she was about to say something, but unusually, she didn't. She smiled back at him, warmly, deciding to say something after all. She was about to ask a few more questions and had taken a breath ready to go, but Llewellyn stopped her in her tracks.

'Well, have a relaxing afternoon, Mrs. Evans.'

'Do you know, Llewellyn, my father, God rest his soul, said that a walk around the village solved anything on your mind. It'll be all right, Llewellyn, lad. I promise. Put it all behind you and move on.'

He nodded and turned back up the hill to Gellia Farm. Mrs. Evans carried on watering her plants.

Reverend Isaac was preparing his Sunday service after a terrible week of events, when there was a knock on the door. Abandoning his preparations, Reverend Isaac went to answer it.

'Ah, come on in, Mr. Tennant. How can I help you?'

The two men were on fairly friendly terms; Mr. Tennant would usually visit when something in particular was troubling him.

'I thought I should come and see how you are, Reverend. It's been a difficult week,' Mr. Tennant began.

Reverend Isaac raised his eyebrows. Not one single person had asked that all week, and it was appreciated. He knew the only other person likely to ever ask was now lay, resting hopefully in peace, in the ground in the churchyard.

'Ah, yes, thank you. I cannot pretend to be all right, unfortunately. This has hit the village hard and I feel helpless.' He rested his hands on his lap before getting up to pour himself and Mr. Tennant a brandy. Yes, it was Sunday, and he really shouldn't, not before a service, but he needed it. They clinked glasses.

Mr. Tennant nodded to the old vicar and said,

'I saw you discreetly positioned in the gallery, so I know you heard and saw it all.' Reverend Isaac nodded as Mr. Tennant continued. 'I'm not one to completely trust Parry but he was right about

Gwen. I hope I can trust you, Reverend, when I say, I think Llewellyn killed Margaret.'

Reverend Isaac was not quick to respond but remained emotionless to the declaration whilst he carefully considered his reply. 'The jury were right that there isn't enough evidence. But I think you may be right.'

'And there was me thinking you'd immediately dismiss my position. You do surprise me sometimes, Reverend. I heard Alice talking yesterday and it seems my staff all believe Llewellyn did it.' Another swig of his drink was taken.

'I've seen Alice a few times now with a chap I don't recognise - is he one of yours as well?' Reverend Isaac enquired.

'Ah yes, that's one of my new canal workmen, Jack. New to the village. Hard worker, and charmed Alice immediately, which is no easy task.' He smiled as the placed the glass back up to his lips. It clinked against his teeth. Reverend Isaac nodded, smiled and mirrored Mr. Tennant's action by sipping his drink also.

'Ah yes. And the canal work is proceeding all right, I assume?' Reverend Isaac liked to know these things, as parishioners asked him about them, even though he was never directly involved in village matters, they knew he would know, so he found out.

'We've had a few structural hiccups, actually. Nothing that can't be sorted though.' Mr. Tennant frowned.

'More costs, then. Is it worth it?'

Reverend Isaac didn't know what he was talking about but wanted to seem interested.

'It will be when it's all completed. I was disappointed by the narrow mindedness of the businessmen in this town, though.' Mr. Tennant remained upbeat. Reverend Isaac recognised when Mr. Tennant was about to get to the point of what he came here to say.

'I'd like to buy a gravestone for Margaret. Only this needs to be like no other gravestone for miles.' Mr. Tennant sat taller as he said this and the vicar raised his eyebrows as if intrigued.

'I'm listening, do go on,' Reverend Isaac replied.

'Even you think Llewellyn might have killed her and I wish to scare him a bit, maybe even into confession. The whole village seems to think he did this, and I'd like to represent us on this stone. I've spoken to someone who is a bit of a wordsmith, that's certainly not I, as I deal better in numbers. But I think a gravestone with the word 'Murder' written on it, facing Gellia Farm would be something in this village.'

Reverend Isaac looked aghast at this suggestion. 'Oh, I'm not sure about that. Mr. Tennant. He's been found innocent and he is innocent until proven guilty, I believe, despite anything anybody thinks. Besides, all the gravestones in the church face the other direction.'

Mr. Tennant, it appeared, was not listening to Reverend Isaac. He jumped up and waggled his finger in the vicar's face. 'Precisely. Imagine the power this stone could have. We could haunt

Llewellyn into a confession. It'd put St. Catwg on the map, telling the world that we will not rest until a killer is found.'

The more animated Mr. Tennant got, the more Reverend Isaac shut down as he waved his hands as if to dismiss the preposterous idea.

'No, no. I am happy to gather evidence and keep asking questions and we'll get there, the right way.'

'You think he did it, I think he did it. The only person that doesn't is his beloved father and possibly batty Mrs. Evans, but the whole rest of the village does. Margaret deserves to be recognised. She made such an impact on the village in no time at all. Let's give her a fitting tribute.'

Reverend Isaac listened, slowly coming around to the idea.

'Margaret does deserve recognition. Maybe you are onto something here, Mr. Tennant.' The grave was currently unmarked, and Reverend Isaac knew that he would not be able to fund anything himself – nor should he for a parishioner as he could not be seen to have favourites and Margaret had already pushed him further than his duty on more than one occasion, alive or dead.

Mr. Tennant was now animated. He patted Reverend Isaac on the shoulder.

'That's the spirit, Reverend, I knew you'd see sense. This will take a few months to get sorted so keep up your detective work in the meantime and keep asking those questions. I'll do the rest.' Mr. Tennant looked distracted.

'I'll certainly think about it, but at the least, she

deserves a headstone.' Reverend Isaac for the first time since the murder, felt he could breathe because of Mr. Tennant's proposal. They shook hands and Mr. Tennant went on his way feeling so much lighter than he had entering the vicarage.

Mr. Tennant was on his way home to Coombe Lodge when he bumped into Alice and Jack. They both should be working, yet both were looking lovingly into each other's eyes. Alice was sat on the wall, twiddling the hair that had escaped her hat and swinging her legs. Jack was stood close to her, hanging on to her every word. They both jumped on Mr. Tennant's arrival and Alice slid off the wall to stand up. Mr. Tennant was not happy.

'Do you both want to lose your jobs?' he shouted. Alice shook her head.

'No sir, sorry sir.' She swiftly ran back into Coombe Lodge not even looking at Jack.

Jack gave Mr. Tennant a menacing hard stare.

'Do we have a problem, boy?'

'No.'

'Good. Get back to the canal. Now.' Mr. Tennant asserted his authority and watched Jack walk behind the back of Coombe Lodge and join the other men working on the canal. Mr. Tennant noted the attitude of Jack and did not like it one bit. He shook his head as he saw Jack resuming canal work and decided that he might need to keep a more watchful eye on him in the future.

Stanley was restless in his home, and sat at his table, his leg twitching in rhythm with his frantic thoughts. There was only a week left of his voluntary time, and he had to make it count. Neither him nor the vicar could have done any more than they already had in the past seven days and were definitely proactive rather than reactive. With youth on his side, Stanley remained optimistic that the next seven days would reveal something further, something significant. He knew that even after his voluntary police work was up, like the vicar, he would remain dedicated to the cause, as long as it took. Even though he had never met Margaret, he felt a moral obligation to do right by her, and the village. It simply would not do that a murderer remained on the loose. Plus, he thought of the respect he would finally gain if he was the one to catch a murderer and see him hang. His status and reputation would elevate and maybe he might even get a girlfriend. Stanley had calmed his nerves and went to bed full of hope and future dreams.

The thoughts at the vicarage were different. With Reverend Isaac's aged mind, he was now struggling to process the enormity of everything that had happened in those past seven days. How he missed Margaret. Whilst his heart told him that there was nothing he could have done differently to try and prevent this or solve the crime any faster, he needed answers that did not seem to be there. He felt the weight of the entire village's expectations on his shoulders. Maybe the vicar's role was easier than that of investigator; parishioner's problems often came and went in a matter of days and were soon swept away as fast as his door open and closed. Margaret's murder investigation lingered, unmoving and frozen. Stanley could forget about this in a week's time, yet Reverend Isaac would have this clinging to him until the end of his life. There simply had to be a resolution. He prayed harder than he had ever prayed before, desperate for some answers for Margaret, her unborn baby, and the village. Justice was needed. With nowhere else to turn, this investigation required a divine intervention. A speedy and conclusive one at that. A clock chimed in his parlour interrupting his thoughts and he knew he had to stop thinking of Margaret and divert his thoughts elsewhere. He sighed heavily but his thoughts went back to Mr. Tennant's gravestone plan and he deliberated it. If something like that would cause such a stir, then maybe he would support the cause; it'd certainly get people talking. No, it was too late in the evening to make such a big decision. That could wait. Finding a killer could not.

Reverend Isaac propped one arm on his chair and lifted himself up. His legs were aching more these days. Despite the pain, a smile crept on his face as he thought about how he regularly saw Mrs. Evans on her daily walk around the village. If he started something like that however, he would have to choose a different time of day, or he'd be put off doing a daily walk if he had to walk with Mrs. Evans. Or she might change her time if she saw him taking a similar route. Maybe he'd have to try laps of the church instead. Once stood up, Reverend Isaac stopped to look out the window. Another thought of Margaret entered his mind with her criticising him that one day soon he'd try and look out and see nothing because the windows were so dirty. She never got to cleaning them for him. The window ledge was thick with dust as he ran his finger along it. However, he was reluctant to admit that he was starting to struggle to see outside. It must have been the position of the candle that made it difficult to see on this occasion. Slowly, Reverend Isaac took himself to bed. His hope was depleting with every step, but his determination would not falter. It could not.

There was simply no denying however, that the path for justice had run stone cold.

Part Three

Chapter Thirty-Two

Gellia Farm, May 2022

Gellia Farm remained virtually unchanged since the Richards family had lived there, two hundred years ago, except for the growth of the trees which now lined the view from the farm to the churchyard. Dave and Tracy, the latest occupants of Gellia Farm, could no longer see the Murder Stone from their bedroom window, although they were used to the occasional visitor wanting to see the farm. A large sign declaring that the property and land were private and trespassers would be prosecuted deterred most onlookers, however, the odd one or two would have the audacity to push a little further. Dave and Tracy cursed Sam Honey and his historical tours, which always encouraged such activity.

A question they got asked regularly was whether or not Llewellyn did flee to America or Canada as the story insinuated through the centuries. Even Sam admitted he couldn't find the answer to that question. The farm had not been owned by the Richards family for decades. No one knew how long they had been gone. Dave and Tracy had bought it off a non-local family who also knew little about it.

'Anything else need bringing up here, Trace?' Dave shouted. He was on a ladder making trips to the attic which they were clearing out, to make room for some boxes of their own that they wanted to store there. It was their first anniversary at Gellia Farm and they loved being there. The village was so friendly, and they felt at home right away, despite being obvious outsiders.

'One last box please, Dave.'

The ladder squeaked as Dave trundled down to grab it. He winked at her, picked up the box and set the steps screeching again as he climbed back up the ladder. Whilst up in the attic, he noticed a dusty, old box in the far, dark corner. It was not one of their boxes. Dave was careful with his footing as he approached the box.

'Trace, can you come here a sec?'

'Why, what's up, Dave? I'm making a sandwich.'

'I may have found some treasure,' he replied, casually. Tracy ran across to meet him at the bottom of the ladder.

'What do you mean, we aren't pirates?' she asked, grinning.

'Ooh arrr, we might be here, my fair maiden!' Dave attempted his worst pirate accent. Tracy laughed.

'What are you going on about, my buffoon?' She gave him a playful shove on the ladder making him wobble. He laughed as he reached the bottom rung and placed the box on a nearby table.

'Treasure.'

The box was old and crumpled - the dust gathered on its lid initially made Tracy cough. The word 'RICHARDS' was written in messy block capitals on the top of the box. Dave and Tracy looked at each other, saying nothing. Dave opened the box. Inside was dusty and delicate, worn with age paperwork. He carefully unfolded the first few documents.

It was the marriage certificate of Llewellyn Richards and Gwendolyn Glebe, dated 1828. There were also birth certificates for Llewellyn, Charlotte, Margaret, Edward and Arthur Richards, their parents were listed as Llewellyn Richards, and Gwendolyn Richards, née Glebe. Children born in 1823, 1829, 1830, 1833. Dave and Tracy read through these documents carefully. Tracy pulled another dusty document out of the box and opened the folded, aged paper slowly, mindful of its condition. It was a death certificate for an Arthur Richards, who died in 1841. Dave broke the silence that had developed as they both read the sad little paper.

'Well, this proves the Richards family were still here in 1841. So maybe they didn't flee, after all, although I can't say I've seen any graves in the churchyard belonging to anyone called Richards.'

'I don't suppose you've ever looked, you crackpot!' said Tracy. 'So, maybe they left after the little boy died. His grave would be here, wouldn't it? That would make sense, wanting to get away from a place where your child had died. I can understand that. But, Dave, they lived here after the murder for what, twenty years or so. What a family. They must have been made of strong stuff. Or Llewellyn must have been innocent, despite what people thought. We should tell Sam.'

'No, let's keep that know-it-all guessing. I like this being our secret, don't you?' He squeezed her hand.

'Yes, I do actually. It's part of our history too, now, isn't it, as we live here on the farm where they lived.' She looked at him with tears in her eyes, but Dave was pleased to see that for once Tracy was interested in the Murder Stone. He took great interest in its place in history, which nearly made them change their mind about buying the farm. In the end, they loved the location so much that they decided the onlookers would have to look on from as far as distance as physically possible.

'What shall we do with this box, Trace?' Dave asked.

'Put it back where it belongs. Its gathered dust long enough, what will a few more years hurt until we leave. The next occupants may have the same surprise as us.'

'Shall we walk and see Margaret?' Dave asked.

'Who?' Tracy questioned.

'The Murder Stone, silly.' He reached over to her and kissed the top of her head.

'Oh. I thought you meant an actual living person. Shall we take Margaret some of the flowers from the garden, then?'

She said. 'Yes, lets. Then a pint in The Crown if you're up for it?'

'Now you're talking.'

Tracy grabbed her gardening gloves to choose some pretty looking flowers for the grave. Dave stopped for a second inside the farm. It was easy to imagine Margaret living here, baby on the way, and her love for Llewellyn blossoming before the pregnancy. Keen to forget the murder part, he felt like it was a happy home. Tracy picked up the daffodils and bundled them together with an elastic band. Dave clocked her flowers.

'Ah, daffy's, great shout, Trace. They'll look lovely.' He put his arm round her, and they headed down the hill.

They both looked at the grave and Tracy popped the flowers down in the pot, when she jumped unexpectedly.

'What was that?' she asked Dave.

'I didn't see anything, love.'

'I thought I saw a – oh, never mind, let's get that drink.' He held her hand and they left the graveyard, heading towards the pub. Dave noticed that Tracy kept looking back; he squeezed her hand.

'Trace, you sure you're okay?' He looked at her, his eyebrows crinkled.

'Yes. I'm great.' The words didn't match the tone. Behind them, the churchyard echoed in the silence and the daffodils on Margaret's grave blew gently in a non-existent breeze.

Chapter Thirty-Three

Gellia Farm, March 1823

Baby Llewellyn screamed, on and on into the night, refusing to sleep. Gwen lifted him up and cradled him in her arms. Llewellyn shouted from the bedroom.

'Keep him quiet, Gwen, will you, some of us have to be up for work in an hour and could do with some sleep.'

Gwen pushed her hair from her face and rocked baby Llewellyn further. She cursed his father under her breath, not wanting yet another argument, as that soon meant that Mr. Richards would get involved. There was no way that was happening again.

It still felt like the middle of the night even though daylight was starting to creep in through the murky windows. Gwen sat in the chair as baby Llewellyn had started to settle. After only a few minutes, both were asleep in the chair until Mr. Richards got up for work and banged and crashed around. The farmhouse, if it was possible, was even untidier than usual with extra baby clothing and equipment scattered across the floor.

'Morning, you two,' Llewellyn chimed, coming into the kitchen.

Gwen blinked rapidly for a few seconds, but as she woke and got her bearings, she sat up and, rocking the baby, kissed Llewellyn. Her eyes stung;

exhaustion like this was unknown to Gwen. Mr. Richards was less sympathetic.

'You have to settle that baby quicker, Gwen; we need our sleep. How lucky we are that this doesn't affect David, or we'd be struggling about now.'

Gwen was about to issue a sharp retort but realised there would be no point. The volume of nighttime disturbances was making Mr. Richards particularly cranky in the mornings, and Gwen realised that it showed on his face as the dark circles had a new shade of dark each day over the past two months. She felt guilty, but where was the support? What was she to do?

'I'm trying, I promise I am. I'm struggling, too. I'm going to visit Mother later to see if she can help me or give me advice. This can't continue.'

Gwen clocked Llewellyn staring from her to his father, it was clear he felt awkward caught between his father and the mother of his child. Gwen did feel loved, but since she had moved in a few months ago, the atmosphere at the farm had been tense. She couldn't deny it. Whilst relieved that a sort of normality had returned to the village, she still heard the whispers about him, the accusations, and felt he could never leave the farm without someone saying something. The farm staff remained loyal, David signed less about Margaret now. Gwen half suspected he used Rosie for that type of chatter. Victoria kept her head down as milkmaid. She was the longest serving milkmaid they had kept in some time.

Gwen sighed.

Another day with the inner workings at Gellia Farm had begun, without Margaret, and with a trial behind them. Gwen saw her days blur and repeat. She remained alone with the baby, as the men did the manual work, day in, day out. She wiped a tear from her face and forced a smile at her son as she held him close to her. Now he was quiet. Another tear dropped. Her mother would know what to do, wouldn't she? She clutched her baby tightly.

Chapter Thirty-Four

Coombe Lodge, March 1823

All the staff at Coombe Lodge worked at speed, accidentally brushing against each other as they passed in the corridors and not looking where they were going. Mr. Tennant was barking instructions to anyone who was prepared to listen to them. He was at his happiest when he was busy, and the numerous projects he had on the go were fulfilling that need.

The canal work was now deep in progress, as was Margaret's gravestone. Having confided in Keep, his housekeeper, he disclosed his intentions for the stone. It was on her recommendation that the rest of his staff knew, particularly when certain writers came at the door begging for five minutes to speak to Mr. Tennant for 'a most unusual opportunity,' as the advert in The Cambrian newspaper had described it.

After Mr. Tennant's announcement to his staff about his intention to buy a stone for Margaret's grave, he observed that they initially provided a mixed response. Whilst most admitted they did believe that Llewellyn had killed Margaret, it was only in the last couple of months that it felt as though the whole village were putting it behind them. With no more killings in the village since, it was clear it was a one-woman attack, and potentially only one motive. Jack spoke up first.

'I think that this is an honourable thing you are doing, Mr. Tennant, and I, for one feel incredibly proud to work for you.'

Whilst others were less outspoken than Jack, the sincerity of his words encouraged the rest of the staff to follow with the exact same sentiment and most murmured their agreement towards Jack and his words. Mr. Tennant knew he had the right team behind him. Jack's team were certainly loyal, and Bryn was still a close friend. There were still one or two that said nothing but did nod their heads in agreement. At least he had a fully supportive workforce.

Florence was the only one who froze during that declaration. Mr. Tennant spotted this, so after dismissing the other staff, took her to one side.

'Why, have I said or done something to offend you, Florence? I hope you can trust me.' Mr. Tennant ensured that the conversation was private by rushing to shut the door.

'Sorry, sir. I can trust you, sir. A lot of people know that I was the milkmaid at Gellia Farm before Margaret Williams, sir. I know that the village are aware that I am now under your employment, but there was some gossiping with my swift departure after only a few weeks at the farm. I'm worried because, you see, Llewellyn did try something with me, only I turned him down. I escaped Gellia before I felt under threat any further. In Neath on some errands for the farm, Mr. Bullins offered me employment at his estate immediately, so I went, wanting away from Llewellyn. Of course, at the time, I didn't know what I was walking into there, either.'

Mr. Tennant for once didn't know what to say. He had no idea. Florence shook as she spoke. She hung her head down, but Mr. Tennant lifted her chin. He was quick to reassure her.

'Florence. I am so sorry that happened to you. Of course, I had no idea and did not even know that you were at Gellia Farm. I am now even more pleased that you are safe here in my employment, and I hope that you are having a happier time here. Let me assure you, that I have my own reasons for doing this gravestone, and although I am now even more certain than ever to do it, that is not due to your actions. Let me reassure you by telling you this, but I will not break confidentiality. There are other people who have their own reasons for hatred towards the Richards' family. The Richards's live above the village and sometimes think they are above everyone and hold some power over others in the village. Not for much longer. Let's see how they feel when those of us below haunt their height. Thank you for your honesty, Florence. It will go no further. May I say, I thought after taking you with me at Mr. Bullins's that you may be a risk, but you and Alice are two of the finest maids in the Neath area and I am grateful to you both for your endless hard work and energy. You are free to go.'

Mr. Tennant opened the door for Florence who, he noticed, had a bit more colour in her cheeks again, and stood a little taller as she left to join Alice and Keep for their next task of the day. Mr. Tennant was even more determined now to take the Richards family down.

Chapter Thirty-Five

Vicarage, March 1823

Reverend Isaac was slowing down in his old age. His joints were stiff; he could no longer recite passages from the Bible and know which chapter they were from; even getting out of the armchair was proving to require a huge effort. The murder investigation took its toll and there was still no justice served. Stanley kept pursuing lines of enquiry to no avail, and with less clues by the day, slowly the village forgot and moved on. Reverend Isaac could not forget.

All this gravestone nonsense stirred up old tensions again that had started to rest. Reverend Isaac had written many speeches in preparation for the Memorial Day, then after only a few lines would believe them to not be strong enough, or sincere enough, or sentimental enough. For once, Reverend Isaac was finding himself lost for words.

Mr. Tennant had visited Reverend Isaac a few months ago, to try again to put forward the idea that 'Murder' should be on the gravestone. Mr. Jones was already at the vicarage that day, the two gentleman having spent more time together in recent months, after suffering Margaret's loss. Reverend Isaac thought back to that surprising conversation.

'You see, Reverend, think of the impact that a

gravestone with the word 'murder' on it will have. Everyone will talk about it for miles, visit the church from miles around, St. Catwg will be on the map.' Mr. Tennant was thinking big again.

Reverend Isaac and Mr. Jones maintained silence for a moment before Mr. Jones stepped in. Reverend Isaac remembered his surprise at Mr. Jones' stumbling start to conveying his thoughts but not getting them out. After a few attempts, he began by informing Mr. Tennant of his mother's circumstances and the motive for helping Margaret. Reverend Isaac was still stunned by that news. It soon became apparent that Mr. Jones had more to say.

'Mr. Tennant, you have my full blessing to do this. Please do it. What neither of you know, is that my mother's story is similar to Margaret's indeed. More than you might think.' He paused.

The tapping of Mr. Tennant's foot was further interrupting the Reverend's thoughts.

Mr. Jones continued.

'Mr. Richards and I are half-brothers. Only Mr. Richards' father chose his wife and abandoned my mother.'

Reverend Isaac sat staring at Mr. Jones who looked nothing like Mr. Richards. After so many years of silence, he'd finally got the words out that he had wanted to say and that had relieved him of his burden. On a close inspection, perhaps yes, there was a small likeness, around the mouth. Mr. Tennant sprang out of the armchair and made Reverend Isaac jump.

'Well, that settles it. The Richards' family cannot keep ruining lives and pretending to lord it over the village because they have the highest farm in St. Catwg. Reverend Isaac, I am assuming, based on Mr. Jones' position, that you will not provide any further objection to a "Murder" gravestone? Mr. Jones, you were brave to tell us that. You can trust that it will not go any further.' Mr. Tennant was resolute, and Reverend Isaac knew there would be no stopping him, no matter what he said.

'I cannot disagree, Mr. Tennant.' Reverend Isaac found himself saying and was shocked at his own reaction. It would be unfair to protest after everything Margaret and Mr. Jones had suffered with that family. Enough was enough.

Reverend Isaac regularly thought back to that conversation over the next few weeks, still finding it hard to believe Mr. Richards and Mr. Jones' relationship. He slumped in his chair, awaiting for the next drama to unfold in front of him. There were always going to be secrets in the village, that much he knew. Many left untold.

Chapter Thirty-Six

Gellia Farm, April 1823

Life was settling down at Gellia Farm. David loved having a baby in the farmhouse. It was weirdly reassuring to him to have someone else in the farm that could not communicate, at least not yet anyway. David had mixed feelings when he was told that Gwen would be moving in. They were still unwedded and he felt it to be disrespectful to Margaret. However, he also recognised that finding alternative employment would be near to impossible, and the Richards' family had treated David as one of their own, despite his disability. If only they could have done the same for Margaret.

It was a crisp April afternoon, so David went outside whilst Gwen fed the baby. Recognising he was now a spare part in the way of family activities, he headed into the garden area. Leaning against the wall, he looked down at the church and towards where Margaret was buried. He missed her. It was such a short time that she had lived in the village, yet he felt like he'd known her his entire life.

Alice and Jack were seen running out of the Crown and down the street, presumably back to Coombe Lodge. Both looked merry, and David hoped that this was their day off or both of them would be in trouble with Mr. Tennant. Jack swirled Alice around at the edge of the graveyard and then they trotted down their usual route in unison.

David smiled as they both looked so happy together. Out of nowhere, David watched Jack bend down on one knee. Alice held her hands to her mouth, nodded and they embraced. No ring was put on a finger, but Jack stood up and swung something around Alice's neck, fastening it up behind her. They continued to make their journey back, holding hands, and skipped down the road. David clutched his hands towards his chest. What a way to be a blissfully unknown witness watching that moment between two people in the village.

He walked back into the farmhouse, desperate to share the moment he had seen, but only Gwen and the baby were there. Gwen had taken an instant dislike to David and had made no effort whatsoever to try and communicate with him. It was clear to him that she'd never match up to Margaret's high standards of thoughtfulness and care in any way.

With no one to share his news, he returned back outside as he hadn't waved goodbye to Margaret. Every time he walked past the grave or saw her resting place from the farm, he waved. There was no way he could forget her. As he lifted his hand, he saw six people, men and women head towards the church entrance. David knew them and knew he saw them regularly, once a week and again on Sundays, but never understood what they did. They made their way up steep narrow stairs to do what? Why did they go upstairs, disappear for a bit, then come back down? He shook his head, baffled at the prospect, it made no sense.

Meanwhile, the new family of three were now cuddled up in the parlour. Llewellyn looked into Gwen's eyes and kissed her on the top of her head.

'Gwen,' he said. 'How did you know I was innocent; how did you trust me?' Llewellyn nestled into her for reassurance. Baby Llewellyn gurgled and they both grinned at him.

'Please don't be annoyed with me,' Gwen said. 'I was in the church when you spoke to Margaret at her grave after your trial. I sort of listened in once I realised what was happening. I didn't want to disrupt your moment, and I am pleased I didn't as it helped us move on. I could tell how honest you were being, so sincere. I knew.'

There was a silence from them both for some time until baby Llewellyn made another noise and caught their attention. Llewellyn thought about what Gwen had admitted. He squeezed her hand.

'Thank you.' Llewellyn realised that in being honest with one woman, he had actually said his truth to two. It was that simple.

Gwen smiled up at him but teased, 'I would like to hear you speak more animatedly to me, though, as you did that day. Please feel that you can say whatever you wish to share with me. I am listening, and I am here.'

'Yes, I will.' For the first time in his life, Llewellyn looked at a woman and saw only contentment staring back at him. He had found the right woman.

Chapter Thirty-Seven

Coombe Lodge, April 1823

There was only one man in Neath that Mr. Tennant could think of that would be able to write such a powerful gravestone epitaph, a fitting enough tribute to Margaret. Lots of men in the local area had heard of what he was doing, but none seemed to grasp its sensitivity quite like the gentleman he had in mind. He only hoped that the same man saw it this way, too. The advert in the local newspaper had brought only jokers and imbeciles, and then word of mouth from friends and acquaintances had led him clearly to one man. Elijah Waring.

Mr. Tennant had invited Mr. Elijah Waring to talk business at Coombe Lodge. The two men knew of each other through mutual acquaintances and had met briefly on a couple of occasions. Mr. Waring had only lived in Neath for a few years, and was well known for originally being a quaker, speaking at local chapels. That being said, Mr. Tennant recognised how powerful his words would be, and potentially with additional intent.

At exactly the second he was asked to arrive, Mr. Waring knocked on the door of Coombe Lodge. Alice opened the door immediately, and said, 'Welcome to Coombe Lodge, Mr. Waring, may I take your coat so that you will be more comfortable?' Alice perfectly executed these words, with precise pronunciation. Mr. Tennant, who had heard her from the drawing room, grinned on hearing her greeting – the hours of time he had spent teaching her this little speech had paid off at last. She'd come a long way.

Mr. Waring smiled at the maid and promptly handed over his things. Mr. Tennant observed that he was a small gentleman, with a pale face and very round eyes. His pink cheeks were slightly flushed from the short walk in the crisp Spring air. He had fair hair, tinged with auburn, that sprung out in all angles. He twirled the wedding ring adorning his third finger of his left hand as he followed Alice into the room where Mr. Tennant was waiting for him.

'Mr. Waring, sir.' Alice announced, smiling, and curtseyed at her employer, before she shut the door on the two of them, as they began their business talk.

A memory came back to Mr. Tennant, of Alice, when she first began her employment at Coombe Lodge, of when she would always try and listen in on Mr. Tennant's conversations to find things out. He realised straight away as she always used to whisper what had just been said. Only it wasn't that quiet. He overlooked this issue three times, and then on the fourth time, opened the door to find her crouched down, ear just the right height and position to eavesdrop and listen through the keyhole. The look on her face at being caught meant he knew she'd never attempt it again. He knew she hadn't. Now, she closed the door and walked away.

Behind the door, Mr. Waring and Mr. Tennant were deep in conversation from the off. They had already exchanged a few letters on this subject, so Mr. Tennant was not required to explain from the beginning what his intentions were.

'And you've now got Reverend Isaac's approval?' Mr. Waring was fidgeting.

'Yes. I'm not in a position to share why or how, I'm afraid, but I can tell you with total confidence, he has permitted this.' Mr. Tennant declared, puffing out his chest proudly.

'Oh, no, I quite understand.' Mr. Waring's nose seemed to twitch like a rabbit on every few words spoken. It made Mr. Tennant want to wriggle his nose too, but he thought it may come across that he was mocking and rude, and he wanted Mr. Waring on side. He could not afford to disrupt the new friendship.

Mr. Waring pushed his glasses back up his nose and said, 'I've created a first draft based on the type of content we discussed in our letters. See what you think.'

He handed him the handwritten scrawl and waited whilst Mr. Tennant read it to himself. Mr. Tennant's mouth moved with the words, but they were not spoken out loud. He read it a second time before folding up the piece of paper and handing it back to Mr. Waring. Mr. Tennant consciously looked blank, not wanting to give away his thoughts on these words. Mr. Waring blinked through his glasses, growing more nervous, the longer the silence was held. Mr. Tennant took pity and made his decision. He'd kept him waiting long enough.

Getting up, Mr. Tennant went to shake Mr. Waring's hand. 'This is exactly the type of thing I was hoping for. Well done, Mr. Waring. Could you write me out a copy and then I'll get my men to carve the stone as soon as possible. What an absolutely brilliant wordsmith you are.' Mr. Waring's mouth opened at Mr. Tennant's response, but no words came out. Mr. Tennant rang his bell. Alice appeared in no time at all.

'Alice, would you take Mr. Waring into my office and ensure he has enough ink and paper for a page of notes, please.'

Alice nodded and took Mr. Waring into another room as instructed.

'Ring the bell when you are finished, Mr. Waring,' she told her employer's guest.

Mr. Tennant paced the hallway. After only a few minutes, the bell rang and Alice retrieved Mr. Waring.

'I don't know how you don't get lost in this house. There are doors everywhere,' Mr. Waring blinked hard.

'Oh, I still do at times,' Alice told him and she giggled.

Alice took Mr. Waring back to the drawing room with Mr. Tennant where the paper was handed over, and another handshake followed.

Mr. Tennant handed something private to Mr. Waring, who bumbled his thanks and made his way to the hall where Alice was waiting to open the entrance door. Mr. Tennant followed to see his guest out.

'Thank you,' Mr. Waring said, once again.

'Thank you, Mr. Waring. It's been a pleasure doing business with you in such terrible circumstances.'

Chapter Thirty-Eight

Outskirts of Neath, May 1823

The stone mason chiselled away his last letter. It was finally complete after weeks of work. He took a step back to examine his creation. There was something so chilling about this stone that he knew it would be his most significant piece of work he would ever make. He hadn't known Margaret but had heard the story from a few miles away. Poor woman. At least he had now contributed to her story in some way. He examined it closer. It was a shame that a huge chunk of it had fallen out mid work, but the fix looked all right. A fiddly rectangular replacement stone meant another new stone was not required. Surely no one would ever notice that, anyway. He hoped Mr. Tennant would be happy now his daring idea had been created. What would the village think? Maybe he should go to the memorial. No, if it was poorly received, he may never recover from the shame. This was a marking of history. To his knowledge, it had never been done before. This could even start a trend. Imagine graveyards full of murder stones. No, he was getting carried away with himself there, it'd lose its edge.

Mr. Tennant came bounding down the pathway and stopped in his tracks as he approached the stone. 'Why, it's magnificent. Better than I could have ever imagined.'

The stone mason smiled as he stepped back to allow Mr. Tennant a closer inspection.

'Thank you, sir.'

'And this was the bit you told me you were worried about?' Mr. Tennant circled the edge of the rectangular fix.

'Yes, sir.'

'I am thoroughly impressed by your craftsmanship and dedication, young man.'

'Thank you, sir.'

Money was exchanged, and the stone mason, just quickly looking at the wad of cash, could tell that it was double what had been agreed. He rushed to put it in his cottage, not wanting to make a fuss as he felt his cheeks flush. They shook hands.

'Will you help me get it to the village?' asked Mr. Tennant, pointing to the stone.

The stone mason nodded as the two men struggled to lift it on the back of the cart. A worker of Mr. Tennant's joined to help them.

'She's heavier than I thought,' Mr Tennant observed.

'That's what you get with the best Welsh quality stone, sir. She'll last for years, decades, maybe even centuries.'

'Then years from now the residents of that village will know what happened to Margaret Williams. Excellent work.' Mr. Tennant patted the stone mason on the back.

The men shook hands again; the stone mason had many jobs piled up but thought his unexpected pay packet had permitted a cup of tea first. He waved off Mr. Tennant, who looked like he'd gained a prize possession, not a gravestone that would haunt the village of St. Catwg for years to come.

Chapter Thirty-Nine

St Catwg Graveyard, May 1823

Mr. Tennant agreed to meet his canal workers at midnight. He had concocted a plan to ensure the shock effect of the murder stone reveal upon the residents of Gellia Farm and the villagers. Not wanting to erect it in daylight, he knew that his team had to be quiet, fast and sharp. He hadn't even told Keep or his other female workers and had asked the men to keep the secret, too.

The men arrived at Coombe Lodge together, round the back of the property. Mr Tennant ushered them into his cart, observing they had listened to his request of wearing dark clothing. Even though it was a short journey to the graveyard, the stone was so heavy that Mr. Tennant had not dared move it from the cart. It was covered in a black sheet, and even he had not dared to steal another look at it.

The horse's footsteps were slow, and Mr. Tennant heard his men whispering as Jack wrung his hands, and even Bryn was fidgeting. He decided to ignore their apprehension and focus on the horses. Their hooves clattered against the bumpy track, eagerly wanting to go faster, but their master keeping them at a slow and steady pace.

Eventually, they arrived and pulled up at the graveyard.

'Only speak in whispers please, we can't wake the

village. Please also tell no one that you were a part of this. I mean it, no one.' These were as stern words as Mr. Tennant could manage, but he could tell the message had been received clearly.

The men hunched around the back of the cart and kept their heavy coats and hoods around their faces. Mr. Tennant was mildly amused at this scenario – what an unusual situation he and his men were in. Is this what being a graverobber felt like? What if they bumped into a graverobber? No, there were none of those in St. Catwg, surely not.

'Slowly does it.'

Mr. Tennant got Jack (likely the strongest) to support the tilting of the stone off the cart and onto the ground. Not one sound could be heard as Mr Tennant mimed what actions he wanted the men to take. Once the stone was off the cart, they all stood around the edge and lifted it.

'Could you have found a heavier stone?' Bryn whispered.

'Only the best for our Margaret.' Mr. Tennant smiled genially, but Bryn had already turned his back on his friend.

The steps taken, much like the horse ride, were slow and steady. Mr. Tennant saw the careful precision and reverence with which the men carried the stone and realised that these men would need a monthly bonus in their pay. They arrived at Margaret's unmarked grave.

'All the graves face this way.' Mr. Tennant pointed down the hill. 'So, we're going to place this stone in the opposite direction. Facing that farm.'

He pointed up at Gellia Farm. The men in unison turned to follow Mr. Tennant's hand and stared in silence, not moving. A noise made them jump from behind. Another stone had fallen from the crumbling church, which was still yet to be fixed. Further rubble followed as small pieces of debris came tumbling down. Mr. Tennant remembered how well Margaret had spoken that evening to save the church. That night she'd even nearly got Mrs. Evans on side, almost. Tomorrow was for her; this was always about her. The fixing of the church had to happen soon, or they wouldn't have a church left.

'Steady now, gentlemen, gently does it,' Mr. Tennant directed.

The men dug hard into the ground to position the stone. No one spoke a word. The men kneeled to position the light so that their fellow workers could see where they were digging, and how deeply. The lantern's candle flame flickered chaotically, like it was aware of the significance of this stone, and the impact it would have for generations to come. The men focused on getting the job done quickly and quietly. Mr. Tennant looked on, tapping his foot. His men were working at speed but to him it felt like they had been at the graveyard for hours. How much longer would this take? He paced up and down.

Despite the cold weather, Mr. Tennant saw that the men were repeatedly wiping their brows and taking deep breaths due to trying to handle the heaviness of the stone.

'Is there a problem?' He stepped closer to the men so they could hear him.

'No, sir. It's just difficult in the dark, I think the lanterns might go out.' Jack was clearly agitated.

'Well then, make haste.' Mr. Tennant stepped away, not wanting to delay proceedings any longer.

'Sir.'

Mr. Tennant turned away, unable to stand the pressure. He rubbed his hand through his hair and refused to watch the men, for fear of putting them off even longer. Seconds turned to minutes; small steps became large paces and Mr. Tennant's hands were wringing incessantly.

Eventually he heard Jack call.

'Mr. Tennant, sir!' He dared to turn around and approach the stone. It was settled in the ground, standing strong and unflinching, facing Gellia farm. Mr. Tennant's workmen were dusting themselves down, keen to get any soil off the clothes that may incriminate them. The lantern swung in front of Mr. Tennant's face so he could read the words now they and the stone upon which they were written were firm in the ground. The stone looked grander, somehow, now it was where it should be, although the workers were too tired to take much interest in the stone now, or its words. The men had bundled themselves into the cart, stretching and yawning. Mr. Tennant smiled. He would await the collective village response. Time for bed, tomorrow would be here soon.

Chapter Forty

St. Catwg Graveyard, May 1823

The sun rose and the village woke up to the day of Margaret's memorial service. This would primarily be to recognise the gravestone but also as an opportunity to share stories of her and honour her memory. Reverend Isaac had already received a letter from Margaret's parents to say that they were not coming to the memorial. They added that they were not sure if they could ever visit the village again as it hurt too much. Whilst he understood their predicament, he felt a further pang of sadness on receiving their letter.

Reverend Isaac had noted how Mr. Tennant had been nonstop with preparations for the day, agreeing also to put on a commemoration after the service at The Crown Inn. It was difficult to know what the village reaction to the gravestone might be, so some drinks afterwards may lighten any tense encounters.

Reverend Isaac got himself ready and thought back to the day of Margaret's funeral. The situation was still so desperately sad, as much as those first few days had been. He adjusted his robes; everything had to be perfect for Margaret. He held his hand out in front of him. It was shaking.

If he was being completely honest with himself, he knew that there would be some negative reactions to the gravestone. He hoped they would be minimal. Reverend Isaac arrived early to the graveyard and located himself in front of the stone. It stood out, facing the opposite direction to all of the other gravestones in the graveyard. A shiver ran through Reverend Isaac's spine as he realised in that moment, that this would mean that Margaret's gravestone was actually positioned at her feet, and not her head. He read the inscription for the first time:

1823
To record MURDER
This stone was erected over the body of Margaret Williams, aged 26, a native of Carmarthenshire living in service in this parish who was found dead with marks of violence on her person in a ditch on the marsh below this churchyard on the morning of Sunday the fourteenth of July 1822. Although the savage murderer escaped for a season the detection of man yet God hath set his mark upon him either for time or eternity, and the cry of blood will assuredly pursue him to certain and terrible righteous judgement.

Reverend Isaac found himself nodding in agreement to the stone. After only a few moments, Mr. Tennant arrived. He looked cheery for such a sombre occasion.

'How do you do, Reverend, lovely day for it. What do you think?'

Reverend Isaac could tell that Mr. Tennant was

hoping for his approval. What did he think?

'It certainly hits a nerve, doesn't it?' Reverend Isaac had now reread the words over a few times. He continued, 'Any murderer I know would certainly feel the heat with this, whoever he may be.' Their conversation was interrupted by the bellringers who, right on cue as ever, signalled the bells for the villagers to arrive, and in they swarmed. Reverend Isaac greeted all of the mourners at the church entrance. David had accompanied Rosie as the Richards family had chosen not to attend. Not wanting to miss out on any action like she had at the funeral, and left pondering what today might bring after Mr. Tennant's words to her last month, Mrs. Evans was in attendance today. All of Mr. Tennant's staff were there – he had made it clear what his expectations were for the day. An off-duty Stanley appeared, ready for the memorial, despite not knowing Margaret. Henry also arrived, staying on the edge of the gathering. A tired Mr. Jones also crept up to the graveyard. It was a large crowd in attendance, about as many as there had been for the funeral.

Reverend Isaac stepped forward, and in doing so, it hid the words of the stone. The crowd fell silent.

'Thank you all for coming today, to remember a lovely lady who spent far too short a time in this village, and in life in general. Today, Mr. Tennant has kindly brought us all back together, to remember her, and to also remind us all that justice still needs to be served.' He cleared his throat. 'Mr. Tennant, would you like to say a few words?'

Reverend Isaac stepped aside. Today, he felt it was not his place to say anymore. Mr. Tennant stood where Reverend Isaac had, and they switched places. Reverend Isaac was pleased that his involvement was now over with. He had got it right in keeping it short, he thought. As he stepped out the way for Mr. Tennant's moment, he saw that Alice looked to be wearing what looked like Margaret's necklace, the one Margaret had got at the fair. His eyesight wasn't what it was, but he knew Rosie would know, so he decided he would ask her to help him as soon as possible.

'I have spent many a day walking past this graveyard lately, whilst on my way to the exciting canal project that I also have ongoing. Every single time I walk past this grave, I felt it was an injustice that there was no stone to commemorate Margaret, and no justice for her, with her murderer never being caught. Today rectifies this to some extent.' Mr. Tennant spoke slowly and paused, before moving taking one stride to the left and revealing the stone to the wider audience. Recognising that not everyone would be able to read the stone, he read its haunting words out loud.

After only a few moments, there was a collective gasp followed by a stunned silence that lasted a few moments amongst the group, broken by Mrs. Evans flinging her walking stick a little too highly, only just avoiding Reverend Isaac's head.

'This is an outrage. An outrage, I tell you.'

She pointed her stick in Reverend Isaac's direction, the congregation swerved out of the way to avoid her. He backed away, taking small steps but she persisted.

'You've let this happen? You knew? You are an absolute disgrace to the Church of Wales allowing this to happen. You have permitted a head stone to be at a not so innocent women's feet to face that farm of someone who has been found innocent in a court of law? Innocent!'

Before allowing Reverend Isaac to respond to her, Mrs. Evans muttered to herself and headed out of the graveyard and back to her cottage. As she had spoken, her walking stick had flung from pointing at the gravestone and up at Gellia Farm.

The eyes of the crowd followed her stick and gasped once more at the audacity of the Murder Stone, as they realised it aligned directly with the farm. Llewellyn Richards would have a constant reminder of Margaret's murder. Was that right? Just because he had been accused, did it make him a murderer? Mrs. Evans was correct. He had been found innocent. Not guilty. The conversation dispersed into lots of small groups. Reverend Isaac said nothing but looked on. The consequences of this stone were being realised at a rapid rate. Had he done the right thing? He was beginning to wonder! But would Margaret agree, he thought, sadly.

David, however, was distracted by something else entirely. After seeing Jack propose to Alice, he needed to see what Jack had swung around Alice's neck. He edged a little closer to the couple, who were stood together.

Margaret's locket.

David rushed back to tell Rosie immediately in sign language. 'M necklace on A neck.' Rosie signed back that she remembered the locket well from that terrifying experience with Mystic Mildred. She approached Alice and tapped her on the shoulder. David looked on, trying his best to lipread the conversation. Alice spun round.

'Hello Rosie, why isn't this a shock? Margaret will be talked about for miles and miles!'

Rosie couldn't stop staring at Alice's neck.

'Yes, yes, a huge shock. I say, lovely locket, Alice, I don't think I have seen this on you before.' David watched Rosie step towards Alice, and grab the locket, holding up the necklace to her face, for further and closer inspection. David couldn't stand not knowing what Rosie was seeing. Was it Margaret's, as he thought? He looked over towards the grave. Poor Margaret. Baby, relationship and life all taken from her in these few months at this village. The least she deserved was the killer to be caught. He went back to studying the conversation.

'Yes, it's new. Jack gave it to me as my engagement present. He is saving up for a ring but wanted to make a commitment to me in the meantime. Isn't it pretty?' David watched Alice clutch it in her hand like a little treasure before letting it spring back to its normal place.

'Why, yes. Beautiful.' Rosie forced a smile at her friend. 'Well, I'd better go back and keep David company, or he'll be feeling left out. Goodbye.' Rosie rushed off to sign to David.

'It is M's, J gave it to A as a present.' She informed him.

'Tell Reverend Isaac.' he replied. She nodded.

Both went off to discuss with Reverend Isaac their latest findings. He was talking to Mr. Jones. Rosie and David stood back waiting impatiently and Reverend Isaac saw from the corner of his eye that they needed to speak to him. David then held back even further and loitered in the background. Even though he was grateful that he couldn't understand what Mr. Tennant had said, Rosie had signed the announcement for him. His stomach knotted and he looked down at the grave as he could not stand the sight of the murder stone. The reaction was still yet to come from Gellia Farm. He never wanted them to leave the farm and see this declaration. Although, it would likely be seen from the garden. David shivered.

Rosie was talking to Reverend Isaac and David was glad of the distraction. He was grateful for Rosie signing this conversation. He knew she didn't want to give any suspicions away in her chat with Alice, but this was different.

'I'm so sorry to trouble you on a day like today.' Rosie was speaking as slowly as she could so that she could sign simultaneously and so that David could lip-read the words also, although it looked like Reverend Isaac was taking a few extra seconds to process what she had said. David saw him squint to follow the conversation but wasn't sure how squinting would help.

'Alice is wearing Margaret's locket from Mystic

Mildred. It is definitely the same one as it had a slight indent on the back and this one does, too. I had to practically yank it off her neck to check. She said Jack gave it to her as an engagement gift. It is Margaret's. Was Margaret's. Jack killed Margaret. He must have done, otherwise how did he come by her locket? Oh, Reverend, I have never been so sure of anything in my life. David spotted it. The necklace, I mean.'

David knew his name had been said and watched as Reverend Isaac nodded and took his time to absorb the information. A deep breath was had by all three.

'I saw the same thing and was going to ask you to check for me. Leave this with me, I'll look into it.' Reverend Isaac looked deeply troubled.

David stepped forward now and Reverend Isaac gave him a look. David was sure they had done the right thing. Everything would now be all right. He thought they had got the murderer but didn't want to believe that of Jack. Poor Alice, too, as she looked so happy that day. At least the Richards family would finally be left alone once Jack was arrested. David looked around the memorial and couldn't believe what had happened here today. St. Catwg needed to move forward. He walked away with Rosie and crossed paths with Parry, who had turned up, looking like he had left the inn rather than was about to attend it. One look at the Murder Stone was taken before he shouted some expletives and fell to the ground. Before anyone could assist, he propped himself up on one elbow.

'I'm well!' he declared, before sinking to the ground once more. To save any further embarrassment, Stanley briskly walked over to him and aided him back to the standing position. With one arm around Stanley, Parry hobbled his way back out of the graveyard, dragging his feet along the ground to get himself home. David wondered how much more could happen in a day.

Mr. Richards, Llewellyn and Gwen remained at Gellia Farm that afternoon. The last thing any of them needed was to bring even more attention to themselves. It took only minutes for Llewellyn to peer out of his window and see the commotion. He could just make out that the stone on Margaret's grave was facing towards the house. There was no-one about now, the reverend and the others having gone their separate ways, so he ran out of the house, across hill and dale to arrive down in the graveyard. He stumbled towards Margaret's grave and took a few minutes to absorb what was written on the stone. Then, he turned quickly and ran back up the hill screaming for his father.

'Father!' Llewellyn bellowed. This prompted Gwen to run into him, but she was interrupted by baby Llewellyn waking up and screaming, so she headed to her baby to calm him down. Llewellyn knew with Gwen distracted, he'd have the support of his father.

Mr. Richards raced up to see Llewellyn.

'Whatever caused that reaction, son?'

Llewellyn pointed outside the window and saw

his father follow the direction of his finger. Then Mr. Richards noticed the position of the gravestone, facing up towards their farm. He went pale, but patted his son on the shoulder, as his son babbled about the words on the stone.

'Let them have their moment, if that's what they want. You were found innocent and the village need to remember that. Putting the word 'murder' on a stone, changes nothing.'

Gwen walked in, holding a sleeping baby.

'What's happened?'

Llewellyn locked his jaw, and saw his father fixated on the floor. Llewellyn saw Gwen look towards the graveyard, and she immediately spotted Margaret's gravestone. She swallowed hard as Mr. Richards told her what was written on it.

'This is unjust, it is unfair and unkind. Reverend Isaac must have known about this. He must have agreed this. How cruel. I hate this village. This farm has been a pillar of this community for decades and you deserve to be treated with more respect than someone who turned up for a few months, got herself into trouble and expects the village to feel sympathy for her. As we were starting to move on, a gentleman with a canal on the agenda throws us back into village gossip, and we haven't even left the farm.'

Llewellyn was surprised at seeing Gwen so passionate in her distress. She quickly left the room with the baby in her arms. Mr. Richards walked off leaving Llewellyn with his thoughts. What a hateful village. Do they all still think of him as the murderer? This was too much. Innocent clearly can't mean what it used to. He realised his hands had clenched into fists as he punched the bedroom wall. The skin on his knuckles cracked.

Chapter Forty-One

The Crown Inn, May 1823

Once the initial shock of the murder stone had passed, the congregation had made their way to their local inn. Conversation was fruitful on the way, and only a few drinks in, talk started to become full of accusation.

Stanley, who was merry after only his first pint, raised his voice for the entire pub to hear.

'Well, it's so obvious who did it, isn't it? It's about time this village made a stand. Three cheers for Mr. Tennant, I say!' He was now stood on a table with his next pint which happened to be sloshing at the sides and spilling over towards Mr. Jones' bald head. Mr. Jones brushed his scalp with his hand and then held it in front of his face. It was damp.

'I think the inn has a leak,' he said. Stanley saw his pint tipping out and supressed a raucous laugh at Mr. Jones' expense. He tried to distract himself by looking over at Alice and Jack.

Without a care who was watching, the two of them were kissing passionately in the corner of the inn. Neither had touched their drink. Stanley whistled and Alice jumped, looking over towards Rosie. Stanley giggled. Alice saw Rosie turn back to sit with David who raised his eyebrows at their indiscretion. Stanley whistled again but Alice was soon distracted as Jack by now had pulled her close again, and was kissing her with ardour.

The landlord of the inn stepped in.

'Have some care and behave appropriately. This isn't the place to show your affections in this way.'

Alice flushed but Jack looked smug. Stanley couldn't help but watch all of this unfold.

'Why, Just Alice, I think we accidentally caused a scene.' He tucked a strand of her hair behind her ear.

'Why, Mr. Griffiths, I think we just did! How curious.' She giggled into his shoulder.

'You are a curious one, aren't you, my Alice? I feel like there should be a book one day about a curious Alice. She'd make for excellent reading. Particularly one as clumsy as you.' He smiled at her, lifted up her necklace and kissed the locket. Like she had earlier, she clenched a fist around it in her hand. Stanley got bored and downed another pint.

Reverend Isaac had decided to go to the inn, after all. Rosie's confirmation of Alice's necklace had been significant. Her detective work only reaffirmed his original suspicion. What a thoughtful gentleman David was, so protective of Margaret, and now Rosie. Reverend Isaac thought back to the necklace. As Margaret did not wear it regularly, it wasn't known if it had been missing from the body or not. But it all fit together, otherwise why would Alice be wearing it?

He spent some time carefully watching the couple who were brazenly embracing in the corner.

Unimpressed with this, at what was meant to be a memorial, Reverend Isaac headed to the bar and had a quiet word with the Landlord. Alice would not stop touching the necklace. Reverend Isaac's fingers were drumming against the table. He decided to approach the couple.

'I hear a congratulation are in order, both.' He shook Jack's hand and nodded at Alice.

'Thank you, Reverend, I hope you can still remember the wedding ceremony words, it's been a while since we've seen one in the village, isn't it?' Alice was fiddling with her necklace. Jack gave the vicar a cold, hard stare.

'Of course, I remember Alice, no need to worry about that. Jack, feel free to stop by the vicarage one day soon when you have some spare time, and we can start making arrangements. It would be good to get to know you better.' Reverend Isaac's stare was now the one that was hard. He went back to his brandy and sipped it.

The door clattered open. In walked Mr. Richards, and Llewellyn. Reverend Isaac, seated by the door, now had an empty glass. He needed a drop or two. He went to stand to get another drink, but all eyes were on the doorway and him. He sat back down. What a bad time to run out of brandy.

'Two pints, please,' Mr. Richards requested. The Landlord of the inn nodded and placed them on the bar without saying a word.

'Thank you.' The landlord said, eventually.

Coins were exchanged and despite the inn being full of people, father and son found a corner near to nobody else.

Reverend Isaac knew that he should approach Mr. Richards and Llewellyn but did not know what to say. He needed a drink. However, Mr. Tennant sat down next to Reverend Isaac.

'Well, I think that went better than planned, what do you think?' Mr. Tennant looked merry. Reverend Isaac had watched him receive lots of compliments and murmurs of agreement with the actions taken place today. There was also much more interest in the canal, Reverend Isaac observed, and Mr. Tennant entered in deep discussions with anyone who was willing to ask about anything concerning his project.

'Judging by the way we are being watched by the Richards men, Mr. Tennant, I cannot be as sure as you.' Reverend Isaac kept hushed tones.

'Ah, I think we had the desired effect, Reverend Isaac. They won't be so keen to keep a watchful eye on the village so much anymore, I know that much.' Mr. Tennant finished the dregs of his pint, and nudging Reverend Isaac's empty glass, offered him another.

Reverend Isaac was glad to accept, 'Yes, please.' He went back to watching his villagers.

It was Llewellyn's turn to get the next pint for him and his father. He approached the bar. Stanley took this as his opportunity.

'Murderer, I don't know how you think you can show your face in here. Have you no shame?' He squared up against Llewellyn, seeming too drunkenly confident, waggling his arms about in front of him, edging for a fight.

Llewellyn stayed calm. 'I wouldn't do that, if I were you. You already made one mistake by getting me arrested and put on trial in the first place, do you want to make your second mistake?' He stood up, looming over the puny Stanley.

Reverend Isaac could tell that Stanley was up for a fight. 'There was enough evidence against you, Parry as good as saw you do it.'

Reverend Isaac looked on as Stanley was now pacing on the spot, shifting his weight from his left foot to his right foot and swaying from side to side as he did this.

Llewellyn rolled his eyes. 'You silly boy. He didn't see me, because I didn't do it. How could I have been arguing with Margaret on the hill pathway, when she was found at the bottom near the church pathway? It doesn't add up. Parry needs to answer these questions, and you should prick your ears up and listen. It suggests to me that he implicates himself. He is the one alone that night walking back from the pub. I was found innocent in a court of law. Innocent. You nearly had me killed. I could have hung for a crime I didn't commit, purely because you got excitable with your fortnight's duty. I am sorry that Margaret lost her life, but I am not her killer. The sooner you and this village accept this, the easier it will be for everyone. If you don't, you will only ruin future lives. Now, not only do I have to live with how badly I treated Margaret, but every day also there is the implication that I killed her because of the direction of the stone. I hope that every single one of you realises what you've done today. An actual murderer remains on the loose, you've given Margaret an undignified stone by having it lay at her feet and all to spite me. I am particularly disappointed in you, Reverend Isaac.'

Reverend Isaac felt the pointed finger directly at him as all the eyes in the pub fell on him again. There was so much he wanted to say in response. Why hadn't he stuck up for Margaret, for one. That was the most he'd ever heard Llewellyn speak. He sipped his brandy. This was going down a bit too easily. He smacked his lips to stop himself from saying something he'd regret. Mr. Richards broke the silence.

'I'm proud of you, son. Let's leave, I don't like the company much here.'

Father and son left the inn, Mr. Richards' arm around his son's shoulders.

The Crown Inn was silent once more. Reverend Isaac looked around. Stanley had sat back down, drowning his loss in yet another pint. No one came over to him. The bellringers had not long entered before gaining accidental front row seats to the face-off between Llewellyn and Stanley. As they hadn't had time before leaving the church, the six of them sat with their pints and put on their rings, which were always removed before a service or practise. To a stranger, it would look odd seeing a group of people slip on their wedding rings simultaneously in an inn, but it was an act that was second nature to them as it would be uncomfortable for them to slide the thick bell rope through their fingers and if a ring caught on it, they could have a terrible accident. Once Llewellyn and Mr. Richards had left, the bellringers and the other villagers swarmed together like bees in a hive, buzzing with the latest gossip and whispering so fast that no one else could capture their inaudible words.

Reverend Isaac spoke to no one and stared at the floor. If today's suspicions became true, it had been a particularly cruel fate for innocent Llewellyn. Mr. Jones headed towards him. He sat down next to him without saying a word. Both men picked up their drink, sipped it and put it back down on the table at exactly the same time. It was at this point that David left the inn with Rosie. Reverend Isaac knew the younger man would want to rush off to be with his employers, particularly after today's revelations, although nothing was proven. He watched David as he signed to Rosie, and they walked out holding hands, without either saying goodbye to Reverend Isaac.

Mr Jones spoke first. 'Margaret had tried so hard to bring this village together and look how her death has broken us apart.'

'I fear today was a terrible mistake.' Reverend Isaac was deep in thought and reflection and the more he thought about this, he felt he had done wrong by Margaret, and the village.

'This is not your fault. Mr. Tennant brought this idea forward, if anything I am to blame in encouraging you,' Mr. Jones replied.

Both men sat in silence but feeling supported in

each other's company for the next couple of hours. There was finally nothing left to be said.

Margaret's memorial was meant to have been a day for reliving fond memories and honouring a woman who had brought life and love to the village in her short time there. Instead, it had become a day of accusations, arguments and a fresh look at who the murderer actually might be. One by one, the congregation filtered out of the inn, and back to their village lives. They headed to their beds to sleep off the many consumed drinks and sleep away Margaret's story. The bellringers were the last to leave as they were forced to respond to the landlord's bell for last orders and stumbled out, feeling wobbly on their legs. The Crown Inn was now empty, rumour less and hushed.

Chapter Forty-Two

Vicarage, June 1823

Only a couple of days after the memorial, but a new month, Jack had arranged to see Reverend Isaac at the vicarage. They exchanged pleasantries and Reverend Isaac invited him in.

'Let me say congratulations to you, once more.' Reverend Isaac smiled, pretending to be thrilled that a wedding would take place in the village, but suspecting the conversation soon to turn sour.

'Ah yes, thank you. Alice is too good; I will not allow her to be set free,' Jack responded. The brandy sips were in full flow.

'Why, what an interesting choice of words you use there, 'set free'? Is she a caged animal?' Reverend Isaac changed his tone.

Jack laughed.

'No, of course not. I like having her where I can see her. You do love your words, don't you, Reverend?'

The mood changed and Reverend Isaac felt chilled. He recognised the spite in that voice and in an instant everything finally pieced together.

'I do hope that you are having your wedding here and not your own hometown, where was that again, Carmarthenshire?' Reverend Isaac was warming up.

'Yes, we will, and no, I'm from Cardiff, opposite direction.' Jack appeared casual, shrugging off the vicar's mistake. Reverend Isaac was unflinching in his reply.

'No, that's what you tell people Jack, isn't it, but you are from the same village as Margaret, aren't you? The nasty fiancé?' Reverend Isaac took a few steps in Jack's direction, positioning Jack against a corner.

'Why Reverend Isaac, in your old age, you must be losing your mind. I have no idea what you are on about.' Jack tried to remain calm but sounded guarded.

'Then why is Alice wearing Margaret's locket?' Reverend Isaac asked, calmly.

'Excuse me?' Jack spat. But there was a strange look on his face, like that of a guilty child.

'Alice is wearing Margaret's locket from the fair, you couldn't get a ring, could you and I now recognise your voice, you were the one who tried to scare me that day at the trial.' Reverend Isaac was swigging back the brandy and getting angrier. Jack squirmed in the parlour corner, his face contorting in an ugly scowl.

'Admit it.' Reverend Isaac shouted.

A long silence hung in the air.

'Yes, yes, it was me.' Jack sank in the corner not knowing where to turn. His eyes were darting but he appeared to be rooted to the spot.

'You sit here and tell me everything.' Reverend Isaac had never been so impatient. 'Now!'

Reverend Isaac pulled up a chair for him and waited as Jack took a few breaths and a few more sips of brandy to calm his nerves.

He'd been caught. He would hang. Reverend Isaac waited for a killer's confession. He was ready.

'The split second I saw her again, I knew I had to kill her. There she was, gliding through the market, basket in tow, looking so fresh faced and, well, happy. We were in love. I knew Margaret felt it, too. Her family repeatedly told me I was like the son they never had. My three sisters adored her. The fits of giggles that came from their mouths whenever they got together proved as much. I was the luckiest man alive.

'And then she left. On the day of our wedding, she flees to a brand new village, miles from home and left. This was completely unacceptable. So, I followed her, never getting too close, as I didn't want her to know I was here. At the fair, I dodged between the crowd ducking and diving because I didn't want my height to give me away. There was a moment when I thought she'd seen me, she seemed to look straight at me, but then, she just shuddered and walked in the opposite direction. I needed to be more careful.

'I wasn't going to lose her again – not twice. I developed a habit of following her and on the day I – the day she died, I followed her. The marshland was squelching beneath my feet, and Margaret was clasping her bonnet and trying to lift up her skirt to avoid the mud, all the while balancing her basket in her arms. I knew that moment was the right moment to approach her. She is alone, and just at that moment, she stops, clutches her stomach and twirls around. She looks innocent, but her body told me otherwise. She was pregnant. I was – saddened – by this fact. And angry. So, I crept up behind her, careful not to squelch in the mud too loudly.'

Reverend Isaac pushed himself to the edge of the chair. He knew this was it. The revelation, the killer! Jack stared blankly at him, looking beyond the vicar to the memory…

"Remember me?'

'Margaret became aware that someone had hold of her. I had crept up behind her and seized her around the midriff. My arm is placed around her neck, pulling her backwards. She stumbles and gasps as she recognises my voice.

'Letting go of the basket containing the sheep's head, she watches it as it tumbles out, rotating and spinning until it hit a rock and stops still, the dead eye's staring without emotion at her predicament.

'"Do you think I wouldn't find you and kill you?' I say, and I know she knows it is I who will kill her. 'How dare you leave me? How dare you!'

'She tries to speak, but my arm is tight around her throat, and she becomes aware that she can't breathe. Suddenly, I spin her around to face me, her attacker, and I push her away to arm's length before grabbing her throat in my large, workman's hands.

'She weeps.

"My baby! My baby!' she manages to splutter in between gasping for breath. She's clutching her stomach as if to protect it, to cuddle the baby she is nurturing inside her. Someone else's baby. Not mine.

'I tighten my grip around her delicate, white throat, taking pleasure in listening to her gurgling, listening and watching as the life drains from her. She keeps struggling; flailing her arms in terror and panic, until there is no more breath left, no more energy to allow her to fight me and she goes limp in my hands. She is dead and I am glad.

'I drop her, dead Margaret, half in and half out of a puddle.

'I rub my hands on my trousers. The air remains as silent as the dead. It's disappointing that I cannot stick around to watch her bloat, but I make a swift exit and ensure I leave no trail behind me…"

Suddenly, Jack breathes and he is back in the room with Reverend Isaac, who has listened to every word Jack had muttered. It was as if he was reliving what he had done.

'You see,' he said, pleasantly to the vicar, 'that would be the biggest crime of all. Getting caught. After everything she put me through. No. never. No more.'

Reverend Isaac interrupted Jack's confession; he felt sick to his stomach and could not stand to hear any more.

'Time for you to visit Judge Woods, boy. You will hang for this.'

Before Reverend Isaac had even put his coat on to head down to Neath with a murderer, Jack took his opportunity and fled out of the vicarage.

Reverend Isaac was surprised to see that Mr. Tennant was stood in the doorway and didn't know how much he'd heard.

'We must capture him. Immediately.' Mr. Tennant's words answered Reverend Isaac's question. Before he could respond, Mr. Tennant flew out the vicarage and followed Jack, around the edge of the church.

He saw rubble fall from the church and clip the side of Jack's head. Jack put his hand to his head, saw the blood, but kept running. Mr. Tennant managed to avoid the rubble and Reverend Isaac moved well out the way in an attempt to keep up.

Jack stumbled and fell down with more rocks falling on top of him. Mr. Tennant and Reverend Isaac could only look on in disbelief as they watched the murderer die in front of them.

'We'll have to bury him.'

'I don't think I can do that. I feel a bit dizzy.'

'You go home, and I'll sort this all out. I think I saw a few graves being dug round the back a few days ago. I'll stick him in one of those, it can stay unmarked.' Mr. Tennant patted Reverend Isaac's back, rolled up his sleeves, and proceeded to drag Jack's lifeless body.

Reverend Isaac got back to the vicarage. The brandy bottle was empty, so he got out another and poured it down his neck as fast as he could. Nothing would settle his nerves. He sat at his writing table and prepared a letter for Margaret's parents. It would have to do.

The letter read:

Dear Mr and Mrs Williams,

I hope that you are both keeping as well as can be. We missed you at Margaret's memorial but can only imagine how hard it must be to even think about coming back to this village. I hope I can reassure you that Margaret is still in our mind, and our hearts. Mr. Tennant's gravestone has murder written over it and points to Gellia Farm. It would not surprise me if you see the words in a newspaper, so please be warned.

I write today with some significant news, and I beg, please sit down if you are not already. There is no easy way to come out and say this. I have found Margaret's killer. At the memorial, you see, I saw another villager was wearing a locket that Margaret sometimes wore in the village. When questioned, she said her new husband to be had given it to her as part of their proposal.

Jack. I am sure that name has haunted you since Margaret had to flee her home. He had joined the canal effort, presumably heard from a friend of a friend where Margaret was and had hunted her down. It seems he could not stand the thought of her not being his, and then the baby news finally tipped him over the edge.

I got a full confession out of him in the vicarage today. He declared everything then proceeded to flee the village. Well, unfortunately my mind nor its legs are what they used to be, and I'm sorry to admit that there was no way of me being able to catch him. That was until he got hit by a stone from the crumbling church and died in the rubble.

I am sorry that this had turned out to unravel some unfortunate events but pray that you and your family now will feel at peace that the killer has been found and dealt with. I pray that Margaret is now feeling safe, away from a man that would clearly never be prepared to let her go. May she now rest in peace.

Yours sincerely,

Reverend Isaac, vicar of St.Catwg's Church.

The letter was stamped, but not yet sealed, and placed on the bedside table ready for him to be reminded to post it first thing the next morning. Reverend Isaac yawned and his eyes felt heavy. His mind was finally at rest, having solved the murder that had been troubling him for months, but his body had given up, and physical exhaustion overtook everything. Reverend Isaac blew out his candle for the very last time, and he passed away in his sleep.

St. Catwg woke up without the knowledge that they had lost their Reverend. The sun crept up out of its shadows and lit the village.

Mr. Tennant was up early that day as he wanted to check on Reverend Isaac after the dramatic events of the day before. He knocked on the door but then noticed it was already ajar. He let himself in and called out to the reverend so he would not startle him. There came no reply. Mr. Tennant climbed the stairs and knocked on the bedroom door before walking in, as he was now concerned for Reverend Isaac.

On entering, he flew over to the reverend's bed, knowing something was wrong for him to be abed at this hour of the day. He took hold of Reverend Isaac's hand, which was stone cold. Dropping the dead man's hand, Mr. Tennant bowed his head and prayed.

As he was about to leave and arrange Reverend Isaac's funeral, he noticed that a letter had dropped to the floor when his coat swung around. Mr. Tennant instinctively picked it up and then saw it was addressed to Margaret's parents. He read it, then spent a few minutes alone downstairs in the vicarage to work out what to do next. Firstly, he would sort out the sorrowful situation of Reverend Isaac's arrangements. He must pay for a lavish funeral; Reverend Isaac deserved only the best. He paced the small parlour, relieved it was he who found the vicar, anyone else and it could have proven to be catastrophic. He lit a candle. The paper curled and blackened under the heat, the truth burning away into nothing. He had a reputation to uphold. It could not be known that he had hired a murderer. Now Jack was in an unmarked grave and out of their lives. Margaret had justice. He would tell Alice that he had sent Jack on a long trip, to cover his disappearance. She may hate her employer, but it was for the best. Mr. Tennant walked out of the vicarage with a detailed plan to protect himself, his employees and his future.

It was settled. The Murder Stone would remain fixed in St. Catwg history forever and no-one except himself, a murderer, a dead vicar and Margaret would know the truth.

Epilogue

The Murder Stone, January 2023

So, now you know. My horrible past caught up with me and stole away my future. Now the latest rumour is that I haunt the graveyard and passersby on route to the canal. I do wander around the canal sometimes; no one can hurt me now. But haunt people? Oh no. I wouldn't want anyone to feel as scared as I did that day after my wonderful trip to the market.

I could not marry him. I knew I was right not to marry him.

I am invisible. No one cares about the woman's body under the stone, who she might be. She could be anybody. They care about the stone. Look what it depicts. 'Murder'. My name isn't Margaret Williams, and my baby never had a name. I am the murder stone girl. And will thus be forever known as such. My death is more significant than my life.

Two days before our wedding, he cornered me and said I was being too friendly with his sisters and not giving him enough attention. He had a nasty look in his eye and that was the first time I felt his hands around my neck. He towered above me. I knew in an instant I had to flee or face physical pain for the rest of my life. I had loved him. We grew up together. From the age of five we knew we'd be wed. Or so we thought. Then almost overnight he switched. I knew of another friend who'd fled to the Neath Hiring fair so sought to do the same. I just knew I had to escape, and fast. I hoped he'd never find me.

I couldn't stay near the crime scene or the village until the day of my funeral. I wondered if he'd have the audacity to show up. The bells tolling in honour of me and my baby were moving and powerful. How I wanted to thank Reverend Isaac for everything he had done for me. Not only was my service beautiful, but I could also see the police making mistake after mistake and Reverend Isaac made it his mission to get justice. It wasn't an easy task, and he remained vigilant and dedicated throughout. My hero.

I was at the stone unveiling. What a stone. They got it wrong though, didn't they. Got the wrong man. I saw a glint in Reverend Isaac's eye when he saw Alice wearing my locket. For an older man, what incredible eyesight. I heard the conversation between my killer and the vicar. What a coward. I knew the Reverend would never catch him as he flew out the vicarage but certainly did not expect what happened next. It was a strange moment seeing him die. Poor Reverend Isaac did not know what to do. An unfortunate incident indeed. But they still blame Llewellyn and the stone is their vengeance.

I watch people visit my stone. I usually lurk behind another stone. There are lots of storytellers who like to listen to the rumours. I've been stabbed, drowned, and strangled. I killed myself and made it look like a murder. I wasn't pregnant.

I was pregnant. It wasn't known who the father was. It was definitely Llewellyn's baby.

I seem to be an enigma hiding underneath a stone. A stone with more words than anyone has ever said about me, my character, my life, my baby. It makes me popular, but only because of one word. One word that hangs over the village, even centuries later. Everyone in this village and the area knows my murder stone. But my name? A few, maybe. In recent years, less and less. Sometimes I am proud that I have a memorable grave, other times I want to be seen as the named victim I am. Mr. Tennant without a doubt did this for publicity, and yes, whilst purchasing my stone was noble of him, I did notice attitudes towards the canals change quickly, almost overnight.

Maybe one day, you'll visit my stone and be the storyteller for the truth, the real Margaret. No rumours, no façade. Margaret. Maybe one day.

Two hundred years and women remain unsafe. Two hundred years and women still lose our lives to the hands of men. Two hundred years and women are violated in their own homes. Two hundred years and women are still joining me in their murdered graves.

The killer may be more easily caught now, but women still get attacked and killed, as I did, two hundred years ago.

I was just walking home.

Authors Note

I was walking past the graveyard in Cadoxton, where Margaret Williams' gravestone stared out facing Gellia Farm. I immediately rushed home and searched for everything about the true story I could on the internet. I had never seen a gravestone declare 'Murder' before! From there, I saw so many misinterpretations and different accounts. More importantly, I saw that the murder was left unsolved. This was around the time of the Sarah Everard case in the press. The reality that both women were walking home, and both ended up dead really struck a chord. Although Sarah Everard's killer was found, the outcome for both women was the same, just two hundred years apart. This led me to look up more domestic violence statistics in the UK where I learned that on average one woman every five days loses their life to a partner or an ex-partner.

With no witnesses and no DNA, it is unlikely Margaret's killer will ever be recognised. I felt compelled to complete this story and wanted to challenge that Llewellyn could be the murderer. He was tried and found not guilty. In the real story, Margaret's father even got him tried again to the same innocent verdict. It was untrue that he and Gwen fled to America or Canada as is widely speculated. Church records from St. Catwg show baptisms of further children between Llewellyn and Gwen years after the murder. Sadly, their first baby did die young, although in my story, it is told slightly differently, baby Llewellyn being their firstborn and surviving.

I hope I have done this story justice, and just as importantly, highlighted how much of a gender imbalance there remains, and is widely unchanged from the last two hundred years.

Bibliography

Church records from St. Catwg Church, Cadoxton. Birth, baptism, and funeral records, from 1820-1840.

The Cambrian newspaper 20th July 1822, 3rd May 1823 and 16th April 1825

1991. Tucker, Keith 'A History of St. Catwg's Church, from earliest times to the present day.'

Griffiths, Martyn, Neath Antiquarian Society website: The Murder Stone Neath Antiquarian Society | Cadoxton Murder Stone

Acknowledgements

Thanks to my mum Debbie, stepdad Nigel, brother Harry, nan Brenda, auntie May and to the rest of the family for your support, listening ear and encouragement.

Thanks to Mark, my friends who have read old drafts, my work colleagues, Neath Little Theatre pals, and my book blogger friends. Special shout out to Sherwood Roberts whose music has kept me company along my writing journey. All your support has meant so much.

A huge thank you to St. Catwg Church, notably Annette Williams, for their support in my research, and even letting me have a go at bellringing, which I am ashamed to say was not my calling.

To get this book where it is now, has taken many fellow author friends. Thanks to Katherine Stansfield, Jon Wilkins, Miranda Dickinson, Tracy Rees, Pat Smail, Claire Sheehy, Bryan Mason, Felicity George, Bridget Blankley, Helen Aitchison, Sarah Watts, Olivia Lockhart, Keith Heaton, Sara Cox and Jennie Godfrey. Thank you all.

Thank you to Jane Murray at Provoco Publishing, who believed in my writing from my first ever short story submission and watched me grow as a writer.

www.ingramcontent.com/pod-product-compliance
Lightning Source LLC
LaVergne TN
LVHW091029080826
845145LV00002B/422

* 9 7 8 1 9 1 9 2 6 3 7 6 2 *